Additional Praise for *Milk Without Honey*

~ ~ ~

"*Milk Without Honey* rings with the truth of autobiography. I could smell the Midwestern harvest, hear the tractor-pulled combine, and feel Ruth Ann's struggle to stay strong in the face of rumors as she fights to lift her parents from their downward spiral. The compelling characters will live with me for a long time to come."
—E.B. Moore, author of *Stones in the Road* and *An Unseemly Wife*

"*Milk Without Honey* has the ring of truth about it. It's a picture of an America strange yet familiar, gripped by Depression, racism, and familial dissolution, yet struggling always to remain decent. If this rural Midwest is not the land of milk and honey, it's a place where the sustaining values—perseverance, decency, responsibility—leaven what's often more bitter than sweet."
—Steven Lee Beeber, author of *The Heebie-Jeebies at CBGB's: A Secret History of Jewish Punk*

"Some of us rural Midwest kids read stories that, when we imagine them shared over a big farm table, are told through the voices of our great aunts and uncles. The stories are about people whose names we forget and dates that blur as we piece the family history together. We wish we had listened more. But what we often do remember—and what *Milk and Honey* offers to the reader—are the vivid details of seemingly benign spaces and objects that tell a simultaneously simple and complex history. In Hoover's captivating book, we absorb the descriptions of photos atop a piano, supper dishes in the sink, and familiar faces gathered on a porch to welcome us home, and we leave the story with hope about family, friendship, and community. "
—Michelle Janning, author of *The Stuff of Family Life: How our Homes Reflect our Lives*

"An alluring debut with vivid descriptions and smart writing that kept me up well past my bedtime."
—Rachel Barenbaum, author of *A Bend in the Stars*

"Here is Ruth Ann, a young girl of the Great Depression, whose memories of her family's struggles with poverty and personal misfortune after losing their farm fairly brim with authentic details of that time and place. As her mother moves the family from house to house in order to survive, Ruth Ann pieces together clues about what might happen next from bits of overheard adult gossip and conversations, 'things that aren't meant to be heard.' Her observations, along with unforeseen calamities along the way, make this lovely story intensely readable."
—Mary Howard, author of *Whiteout* and *The Girl with Wings*

"Reading Lorene Hoover's *Milk Without Honey*, I called to mind the best qualities in Charles Dickens' and Willa Cather's novels. On every page, the novel's unforgettable narrative voice transports the reader into the roaring and flooding and barely survivable—and at last baptizing and redeeming—river of the protagonist's memory. At the center of her family's Depression-era story of diminishing hope, displacement, and hunger, is Ruth Ann's mother, an authentically heroic woman bravely claiming her autonomy while guiding her family towards a new shore. I recommend reading this book aloud to family members, young and old, who are ready to be brought under the rare spell of a master oral storyteller."
—Kevin McIlvoy, author of *At the Gate of All Wonder*

"In *Milk Without Honey,* Lorene Hoover's young storyteller, the ever-vigilant Ruth Ann, opens a secret door to Iowa during the Great Depression with clarity, heart, razor-sharp observation—and the 'gotta-know' infused on every page. I love this book and will recommend it with the same proselytizing vigor I previously reserved for my all-time favorite: *A Tree Grows in Brooklyn."*
—Randy Susan Meyers, author of *Accidents of Marriage*

"Lorene Hoover's child narrator is reminiscent of Harper Lee's Scout Finch: unafraid of reality, always watching, and understanding more than the grown-ups around her think she does. Hoover is a keen observer and storyteller who recreates dustbowl Iowa in deft strokes, navigating poverty, tragedy, scandal, and the fragility of childhood. *Milk Without Honey* is an evocative page-turner."
—Kate Southwood, author of *Falling to Earth* and *Evensong*

MILK WITHOUT HONEY

A Novel

by
Lorene Hoover

LORE PRESS
Boston, Massachusetts

Library of Congress Cataloging-in-Publication Data
Names: Hoover, Lorene, author
Title: Milk Without Honey / Lorene Hoover
ISBN 978-0-578-82866-4 (hardcover original)
ISBN 978-0-578-82867-1 (e-book)
1. Great Depression—Fiction. 2. Farm life—Fiction. 3. Domestic fiction.

Cover Design by Rebekka Mlinar
www.rebekkamlinar.nl

Publisher's Note:
This is a work of fiction. Names, characters, places, and incidents either are the product of the author's imagination or are used fictitiously, and any resemblance to actual persons, living or dead, events, or locales are entirely coincidental.

To the Marshall Family

PART ONE
THE ROAD TO CENTERVILLE

Chapter One

BANKRUPTCY

All that morning in a room heaped with our mother's belongings not a word was spoken about our childhood.

The barren floors and ghosts of pictures that once hung on the walls quieted the four of us as we sorted through what our mother had left behind—some as inconsequential as newspapers and magazines, others as personal as a print dress with her scent and a trace of flour or bacon grease.

She had died on March 1st. Our older brother reminded us it was moving day.

Growing up in a rural Iowa still shadowed by the Great Depression, we knew about moving day. March 1st had often marked our lives, moving as we did from rented farm to rented farm in time for planting. We children seldom saw the landowners, but our stories about life on those farms were built on their names: Faber, Edwards, Dye. No names were given to two of our moves, and we told no stories about those places. At least not in our parents' lifetimes.

Now in mid-March the morning sun shone mercilessly through the windows on things not eligible for an estate or garage sale: cookbooks stuffed with recipes from church friends, mismatched dishes, graceless figurines, and scratched phonograph records. Occasionally there were surprises. In a jumble of dime store jewelry were two fine broaches. "From Aunt Belle, no doubt," my sister declared. I held up an old school slate. "Remember this?" My brothers were more likely to dig out a one-legged doll or an old license plate. "Why would she keep these?"

A stack of worn *Etude* magazines caught my eye. I saw again my mother's work-roughened fingers smoothing an open page before they went to the piano keys. Mixed in with seed catalogs, dress patterns, and birth and death announcements were my mother's letters, journals, and old photograph albums.

My siblings showed little interest in plowing through these more personal affects—especially anything that dealt with what had gone on *before*. Was I the only one who remembered?

Later, away from the tumbled remnants of my mother's life, I flipped through the albums. I was struck by a faded snapshot of me as a four-year-old standing on the porch of a house we always called "the bungalow." I had seen this photo many times, but now with my mind alive with questions it took on a new meaning. Back in 1934, something had happened on that porch. That must have been when it all began.

~ ~ ~

Picture me, my four-year-old self, grabbing my stuffed "Kitty" as soon as my grandfather drove into our lane. I ran barefoot onto the porch, ignoring the night's carpet of dust my mother had not yet had time to sweep away. Beyond the maple tree already dropping leaves, my grandmother in the passenger seat turned to her husband and spoke. My grandfather opened the car door, but sat for a moment. Finally he stood, closed the door behind him as if thinking of something else, and crossed the dry grass to our house. I did not run to him. His hesitant steps were different from the strong man I knew, the one quick to swing me high in his arms.

My grandfather reached for the porch rail, and his knuckles went white. His dark Sunday suit hung shapeless on his tall frame as he stood rooted to the lower step. His straw dress hat shadowed his eyes. His shoes showed scuff marks. Many a Saturday night I had watched him polish his shoes for Sunday church before he saw to it that I polished mine. But this wasn't Sunday.

My grandmother was not one for waiting. Giving the car door a quick shove, she brushed past her husband, and with barely a glance at us, bounded up the steps. My mother holding my baby sister had just stepped outside.

My grandmother was also dressed in her Sunday best—the dark crepe she wore summer and winter and the little hat with its wispy veil. But she was not wearing her Sunday face. What she had come to say had nothing to do with church. She probably wanted to lambast my father, but as usual, he and my brother Frankie were off somewhere in the truck, so it was my mother whose face fell apart at my grandmother's words, sharp as pointed sticks.

"Well, it's gone. This farm we paid out good money for. The bank took it away. Eighty acres from us too. Tell that husband of yours what he cost us."

My mother did not move from the bungalow's doorway. Her apron, stained with baby burp and breakfast grease, seemed to pull down at her narrow shoulders. She brushed a dark sheaf of hair away from her face and boosted my baby sister higher in her arms. "Dan tried."

"Sure he did. When he wasn't running around."

My mother said nothing.

My grandfather's voice came from a low place. "Delia, that's enough." I had never heard him call my grandmother that before. He turned from the porch, his feet dragging across the parched grass. He climbed into his dusty Nash and sat, head bowed and waiting.

My mother was almost as tall as my grandmother, but standing there on the porch she shrunk under my grandmother's gaze. I squeezed Kitty more tightly. Nothing moved. Not even a leaf on the maple tree my parents had planted the first year of their marriage. My grandmother didn't move either. Her eyes were locked on my mother and baby sister. Slowly, the anger drained from her face. Without a word, she turned and left.

~ ~ ~

Did that really happen? Through all these years, no one talked about it. I look again at the snapshot of me on the bungalow porch, holding a toy made by a kinder grandmother following the birth of my baby sister. But I do remember my grandmother dropping snide remarks against my father over the years. I also remember Frankie's story about our father telling our grandfather, "There's no money. I can't pay the mortgage."

Then there are the images of my parents loading chairs, bedsteads, and mattresses onto my father's truck to drive to a square red house close to the railroad tracks where gardens and crops shriveled and died. The following year, they loaded those chairs and tables again, still scarred from the first move, to live on another farm farther away.

But that's how things were before those stories about my father and other women started, before that terrible threshing accident convinced my mother to do something that sent neighbors to their phones and kept party lines buzzing. Years later, I'm still not sure whether my mother's action was foolish, courageous, or just desperate.

Chapter Two

FALL

By the time I turned nine, I should have known things were out of kilter, as my father would have said, but of course no one was thinking about him then. I certainly should have known something was wrong when my sister Nancy and I emerged from our schoolhouse that October to find our grandfather waiting on the dirt road next to his dusty Nash. He didn't call out to explain why we would not be going to our parents' house. He just turned his straw hat in his large hands, his head a freckled ball in the afternoon sun. Eventually he said, "Your momma sent me to pick you up," and we drove to his farm a skip and a jump north of the Missouri line.

Our grandmother greeted us with tight hugs and a grim face. "Your mom's got a lot on her mind right now. She doesn't need four young'uns underfoot. Sure hope your brother Frankie will be some help to her, looking after baby Larry and all."

Something strange was going on, but I was glad to be at their house. At home our parents were always arguing. And our grandmother served better food. My mother's old room had flowery wallpaper and a soft rug. A photograph of a dark-haired girl at a piano stood on the dresser. The girl was my mother, her hands spreading her white dress across the bench. She looked proud and pleased with herself. As I snuggled beside Nancy under fresh ironed sheets, I thought about that photo. My mother did not look like that now.

The next morning the smell of sausage and biscuits woke us. My grandmother's angry voice stopped my rush to the kitchen. "How Sarah will manage, I'll never know." She broke eggs into the hot sausage grease that popped and sputtered on the wood-burning range. "Uprooting these children. You should've talked her out of it."

At the table, my grandfather looked up from his *Capper's Weekly*. "And how was I to do that? You know she don't listen."

"Suppose not. Not after that huss…." Her mouth clamped shut when she saw me. Nancy, only six, padded across the clean linoleum to snuggle against my grandmother's long and sturdy legs. All Nancy got was a gentle push to the table. "Your oatmeal's dished up. Eat it before it gets cold. Ruth Ann, set the sausage and biscuits on the table, while I finish the eggs."

So this was going to be one of those "get things done" days. I did as I was told before taking my place next to my grandfather, a tall, big-boned man with bushy black eyebrows. He must have finished his milking and chores early because he was dressed in shirt and pants for town instead of his usual overalls.

"A lot in the paper about that Hitler fella," he said.

My grandmother clunked the teakettle down on the stove for washing up later. "What's he got to do with anything?" She brushed flour off her apron. "We got enough trouble here."

By now the autumn sun shone through the curtains and drew lacy patterns on the opposite wall. He laid aside his paper and reached up to the gaslights above the table. With a hissing sound, they blinked off. No one else I knew had gas lights—lights that you turned on or off instead of the kerosene lamps that flickered and smoked their glass chimneys. He ducked his head to repeat the prayer he said before every meal:

> *OurheavenlyFatherthankyouforthisfoodBlessittothenourishmen tofourbodiesMaytheworkofourhandsbeeverfavorableinThysightand wedogiveyouthepraiseAmen.*

He had barely finished before he scooped large bites of sausage and eggs into his mouth.

Nancy looked at the oatmeal mounded high in her bowl. "Do I have to eat my cereal?"

"You'll need it. This is going to be a long day." My grandmother sat, her lips pursed. "Lord knows how Sarah will feed these children."

I reached for the large pink pitcher of milk on the table. That caught my grandmother's attention. She had told me once it was something called "Depression Glass." I wondered if that meant it was for poor people. Her lips went tighter as I steadied the pitcher with both hands and poured the milk over my oatmeal. I downed a couple of mouthfuls before spreading a biscuit with butter and jam made from the grapes in her garden. A splotch fell on the tablecloth, and I stiffened, sure to catch it. Instead she took a deep breath. "You girls are going to be moving into a different home today." My grandfather's fork stopped midway to his mouth. She went on, "Your mother's moving you into Centerville."

I couldn't believe it. My mother always talked about how great it would be to live in town, but my father came back at her saying, "I ain't moving to no town."

"In town? But Dad said…"

"Yes, in town. We'll be taking you up there pretty soon, so finish your breakfast and get yourselves dressed."

"Why do we have to move again?" I asked.

"Your mother will have to answer that. Go on, now. Help Nancy for me."

Nancy could help herself, I decided, so I poked along through the dining room trying to figure out what was going on. Overshadowed by the wrap-around porch, the room seemed especially dreary that day. Only Mickey, my grandmother's pet canary, gave it any color. I stopped to feed him in his cage near the window. I wasn't supposed to do that—not without my grandmother standing at my side. I shook some birdseed into the cup, and Mickey promptly fluttered from his perch to peck at the food. It was okay, I told myself. Mickey was hungry.

If we moved to Centerville, when would I see our grandparents again? Would my grandmother still have big family dinners when Aunt Belle and her doctor husband came for a visit? Would we be invited?

My grandmother brightened the dining room for those dinners with a long white table cloth and her shining dishes. Mother dressed us kids in our Sunday best and told us to mind our manners. Nancy and Frankie squirmed on stiff chairs waiting for fried chicken and mounds of mashed potatoes topped with butter, while I watched Aunt Belle, her rose-tipped fingers gesturing as she talked about their new house. To me, Aunt Belle was the prettiest lady ever. My mother's brother, Uncle Stu, and Aunt Violet usually arrived late, and my grandmother was likely to pounce on her, demanding to know what on earth she had been doing. My father, on the other hand, hitched his body restlessly as he listened to talk about town life. He told none of his usual stories. Instead his eyes moved over Uncle Lars' pale face. It came to me now that when my father had dropped us off for the last family dinner, he hadn't stepped foot inside the house.

We were moving again. I couldn't imagine my father changing his mind about living in town. Neither of my parents had said anything about it. Of course my mother was like her father, not much of a talker. She was always busy or lost somewhere in herself. When I'd come home from school, she would take off to work in her vegetable garden or to tend the chickens, and I'd get stuck with watching Nancy and baby Larry. Frankie was never a help. At fourteen, he thought he was too big to hang around the house except at mealtimes, same as my father I guess.

Nancy managed to get her dress on backwards, so I had to help her after all, and my grandmother checked us over before we left. Her comb drew sharp lines through our dark brown hair, but there were tears in her eyes as she smoothed my bangs. Finally she crowded us into our grandfather's car, along with a crate of eggs and baskets of food. As we drove past the orchard and onto the dirt road, I turned back to the petunias and marigolds blooming like a flowered apron along the front porch. Centerville seemed far away.

Farther along the dirt road, we bumped across railroad tracks. My grandfather slowed as we passed the cornfield on the other side. He was especially interested in the blanched husks, their golden silks now dry, brown beards, bent away from stalks ready for harvest. That field had once belonged to him. His lips went straight as he turned onto a gravel road, leading us past a small bungalow nearly hidden by bushes and trees.

Was that the sunken porch he had come to years before? Was it where I had stood clutching a stuffed toy? I studied the torn screen door, the chicken house outside the back gate, and the mottled reddish barn on the rise beyond. I supposed I had been born in that house as had my brother Frankie and sister Nancy. I tried to remember the inside, but it was like a dream lost upon waking.

My mother had spoken of her "bungalow" often. Listening to her stories of painting the walls, making curtains, and planting her first garden, I pictured it a happy place. Just driving past was enough to upset my grandparents. The house had remained empty, the barn's haymow gaping, the garden growing up in weeds, and a rotting circle of pears fallen under the scraggly tree.

"If the bank," my grandmother gave the word hard edges, "had to have the place, you'd think they'd take care of it. Pretty soon the hoboes will take it over."

My grandfather nodded. "I see them every once in a while along the tracks."

I had heard about hoboes. Scruffy men wearing clothes too big for them, they would beg for food from people who lived near the tracks. My mother had grumbled that my father was overly friendly, asking questions about where they'd been, those hoboes filling up on her cornbread and beans all the while. Later she declared they had marked the road, leading a string of others to our door.

My grandmother turned to take one more look at the house. "This wouldn't be happening today if only Dan and Sarah could've hung onto the place."

"You know what hanging on got us."

"Dan could have worked harder."

"Maybe."

"Maybe nothing. He was playing around and you know it."

He made no answer to that, and we rode along the gravel road quiet like. Moving meant Nancy and I would have to change schools again—just when we were getting started good in our country school with a new teacher. I liked Miss Alta. She was young and pretty and quick with hugs. She was smart too. When some of the big eighth graders thought they would have some fun with her—like putting a dead mouse in her desk drawer—she only laughed saying the dead thing showed it was cleaning time and how glad she was that the boys wanted to stay after school to help.

I'd probably never see Jerry from the next farm over anymore. He wasn't so bad even though, walking home from school, he once chased me with a snake. I got back at him by swinging my dinner pail at him. I didn't mean to hit his head.

We were still a good ways from Centerville when my grandfather stopped at Perkins' Grocery in Littleton. Only a few other cars were parked along Main Street, a couple down by the bank and drugstore, another headed halfway into the town garage. Across from Perkins' store, the water tower stood on a weedy lot, streaks of red paint—GO BULLDOGS—close to blocking out the name of the town.

"Grandpa will carry the case of eggs around to the back," my grandmother said. "I have to buy some coffee and flour. You girls stay here."

But Nancy and I were already tumbling out of the car, close behind as she entered the general store. The entry side held little interest for me—wall racks and tables offering a dull mix of men's clothing in black, navy and brown and the everyday blue work shirt. Maybe that was why men liked those big red handkerchiefs.

From weekly trading visits with my mother, I knew that the back of the store held dresses, yard goods, thread, and ribbons, but my grandmother's quick steps, ringing out against the wood floor and echoing up to the high tin ceiling, told me there was no time for dawdling, as she called it.

A broad front window filled the grocery side with light. Close to the window were barrels of apples and potatoes and another of peanuts. Hanging next to a stalk of green bananas was a yellow sticky flycatcher dotted with dead flies. Throughout the grocery side, all kinds of smells mingled, but my favorite came from the coffee that Mr. Perkins ground behind his counter.

There were always people hovering around that counter. On this day as luck would have it, Mrs. Olson waited for Mr. Perkins to weigh out some potatoes. I would have used the back door with my grandfather if I had known I was going to run into Mrs. Olson. Her Tommy had flunked the year before, so he was in my grade again at the country school. He always pulled my hair, and he was stinky like he'd missed his Saturday night bath. The Olsons lived on a small place over the hill from the farm we now rented. My father said he didn't know how anything could grow down in Olson's hollow—all rocks and tree stumps.

Mrs. Olson hailed my grandmother as if she were a long-lost friend, but my grandmother barely paused. "I have to go to the back to settle up for the eggs. You girls wait here and don't bother anything."

My grandmother walked away, but Mrs. Olson stood there shooting looks at Nancy and me. Maybe she was afraid we were going to snitch something—as I had seen her Tommy do. I grabbed Nancy's hand and pulled her past the bins of flour and sugar, past the meat counter where it smelled like something gone bad. We stopped in front of the glassed-in candy case, my mouth watering for lemon drops, peppermints, chocolate stars, vanilla creams—just out of reach. I doubted my grandparents would buy us candy.

While Nancy and I waited, Mrs. Olson stopped staring at us long enough to tell Mr. Perkins that he should add another slice of bacon to round out a pound. She gave us another look, shaking her head. "Poor girls."

I didn't know what she was talking about, and I had no time to figure it out because my grandmother came back to the counter and told Mr. Perkins she needed some flour and sugar.

Mrs. Olson edged in close to her. "When we gassed up at the station this morning, Jim Kimball told us Sarah's moving into Centerville."

"Hmm," was all my grandmother said.

"Dan stopped by our place yesterday morning. He didn't say nothing about moving."

My grandmother turned to Mr. Perkins. "I need a pound of coffee. Will you grind up some for me?" Over the whirr of the coffee machine, she said to me. "Your grandpa's in the car. You two, go and tell him I'll be out in a minute. Go on."

We had to wait longer than a minute, but when she finally approached the car, my grandfather started to get out to help her. "I'll manage." She bundled the packages into the front seat with her. "Let's go."

It wasn't until we had driven the length of Main Street, past a lot of houses that looked as tired as the bungalow where we used to live, that my grandmother spoke again. "Well, the talk has started. That Olson woman couldn't wait to get in her two cents' worth."

"That's just Blanche," my grandfather said.

"It'll get spread around real quick. She'll make sure of it. If there hadn't been all those tales about Ben and that huss…." There was that word again, lost in a slight hiss.

"People shouldn't tell tales," Nancy said. "They're lies, aren't they, Grandpa?"

"Tales are told by people who don't know what they're talking about," he said. "Pay no attention to such talk." The car sped up.

Nancy wiggled around, and her shoe scraped hard against my leg.

"Quit it!" I said.

"I don't have any room." She flipped back the lid of a basket jammed between the seats. It was full of jars of green beans. "Grandma, we got green beans."

It was funny that my grandmother was taking more green beans to my mother. Hadn't we already canned bushels of them?

Clouds had overtaken the early morning sunlight. It was hard to tell where dry pastures ended and sky began. As we picked up speed, fence posts bumped into each other and fences became blurry lines, except at the top of cemetery hill. There, heavy scrolled gates leading into the cemetery broke the lines. Above the gravestones, dark, scraggly pines rose high like black-cloaked figures. I pressed my forehead against the window and closed my eyes.

Chapter Three

THE SUMMER BEFORE

"Paper says the 'dirty thirties' are ending," my father said one night at supper. "Little they know." I wasn't convinced either—not on this Iowa morning when dust blew through my open window. It was bad enough having to sleep in a hot upstairs room—even worse with my sister beside me, throwing off heat like a stove. I kicked against the sheet tangled around my feet. Nancy rolled into the only cool spot on the bed. I pushed her hard. She didn't move. When Larry started crying in my parents' room, I gave up. It was my job to get Larry out of his crib.

I was hoisting him into his high chair when the screen door banged shut behind my mother as she stepped into the kitchen carrying a basket of green beans. Blinking in the dim light, she shrugged off her sunbonnet to let it hang from her neck. Drops of sweat edged dark strands of her thick wavy hair.

"Good girl, you got the baby up." She crossed the sloping floor to the cistern pump and sink.

"He was crying."

Nancy edged in, "I helped change his diaper. It was stinky."

"I'll have to boil water for those later." My mother swung the basket onto the counter next to the water pail. She untied her bonnet, threw it on a chair, and leaned against the counter to take long drinks from the water dipper.

The counter was a fairly new addition to the kitchen. I remembered when the room had been a back porch with rusty gashes in the black screens. Shaffer, the man we rented this farm from, didn't care what fixing up my folks did to the buildings, as long as it didn't cost him anything. My mother probably would not have waited for permission anyway. She was set on getting the porch boarded up and floored to give our family of six "some breathing room." After fussing with my father about needing a sink and cupboards, she finally gave up and built the cupboards herself since, as she pointed out, my father seldom picked up a hammer or saw except to work on some old car or tractor. When she got boards pounded together for her cupboards, she asked him to at least help her hang and nail them in place.

He did that, and if he noticed their rough finish or ill-fitting shelves and doors, he didn't say anything. My mother slapped a thin coat of varnish on them and said they were makeshift like everything else, especially the sink with its ten-gallon bucket to drain into. She sewed a little curtain to hide the bucket that frequently overflowed. The curtain didn't cover the sour smell.

My mother dropped the dipper back into the water pail and went to the wood range, a big hunkering black thing, already making this hot morning a good deal hotter. She lifted one of the lids to check on the fire, letting loose a whiff of smoke. "I'll need more cobs. You girls run out to the barn get me some, okay?"

"That's Frankie's job," I said.

"I'm sure your dad rushed him to get out to the field. Go on, now." My mother turned to Larry in his high chair. "Hello, baby boy." She lifted him out and sat down with him at the oilcloth-covered table, resting her cheek against his downy head.

Barefoot, Nancy and I ran to the barn that stood tall with a steep gabled roof pushing down on tired walls. The barn needed painting, as did the house and other buildings.

The barn was a place apart, wonderfully cool after the hot kitchen. Dim and soft, it had its own scent, a mixture of new hay and manure, churned into the dirt floor by the hooves of horses and cows. In the shadowy interior, curtains of dust twisted and turned before chinks of light shining through the siding.

Near the hay chute, a ladder led upward to the loft. I wasn't as brave as Frankie who would climb up and swing from the barn rope high over mounds of hay. But then he was a show-off. Nancy and I settled for jumping in vast cushions of hay and watching dust motes spin and dance in shafts of light from the open mow.

Startled by our entrance, pigeons flitted back and forth, bumping against walls, their gray and white wings brushing against the uppermost reaches of the roof. One time when my mother had been with us, she said maybe the birds were frightened to find themselves closed in away from the sky.

Finding corncobs for the stove wasn't easy this late in the summer. Soft pinkish-red cobs piled high next to the grain bin the previous fall had now dwindled to a dry, brown scattering. I didn't want to touch those smeared with manure left by cows as they meandered in to be milked. By the time Nancy and I had filled our basket and gone back to the house, our mother had pulled a chair into the back yard under the wide-spreading elm tree and was at work breaking beans. Larry lay kicking on an old blanket stretched on the ground. My mother handed me a pan, and we sat down on the stoop to help.

I didn't mind helping with the beans. I liked the fuzzy feel of the bean pod as I pinched off the tails, and the quick snap the pod made when it broke just right. The best part was working together under the shade of the old elm and coaxing my mother to tell stories. My favorite was about a pie supper she had gone to as a young girl.

It must have been a big night in her country school. I tried to imagine it—kerosene lamps hung in front of mirror-like disks making the light especially bright, parents trying to squeeze into those little desks. Did my mother, like most girls, wonder who would buy her box meal, or worry about the shame if the box sold for a low price? Worse yet, if her father had to buy it?

"Mother made me a dress of the softest white cotton," she said, her face going soft. "It seemed to float around me. And I had a big white organdy ribbon for my hair. It was long then, reaching half way down my back."

I knew how pretty she must have looked because I remembered the picture of her in that dress in her old room.

"I tried to make my box special," she went on. "But of course, Mother insisted on helping me. She made the pie too. Peach, it was. Daddy grew peach trees—no one else had peach trees."

With the back of her hand, she brushed a fly from her cheek. "All the boys bid on my box. Your dad kept on bidding until he got it. I learned later he had to borrow money from his friends."

I could see him, dapper in vest and tie, sure of himself, but I couldn't imagine my mother flushed and giggling in a ring of boys.

"A long time ago, that was." She stood up, grabbed the basket of cobs for the fire, and went into the house.

Lorene Hoover

She came out carrying two water pails. "I need more water. Keep Larry on the blanket, will you?"

My mother started down the path behind the house, her shoulders drooping as if the empty pails were heavy. Her homemade cotton print dress hung loose and shapeless to her bare knees. Her flat shoes slapped the dusty path as she opened the gate, walked past the chicken house, and out of sight to the windmill.

Nancy did a lousy job with her beans. Some she twisted until they were squashed, or she threw beans, stems and all, into my pan. I tossed them back at her to do over again. Nancy said she didn't care and flounced off to sit next to Larry, poking at him to make him laugh or cry. I don't think she cared which. Soon after my mother came back down the path, water sloshing from her buckets. I picked up my dishpan full of snapped beans and went into the kitchen. Steam, thick with the smells of burning cobs and cooking beans, rose from a large tub of boiling water to wrap around me like a hot wet towel.

My mother had kicked off her shoes to work at the sink, washing more beans to stuff into Mason jars. She scattered a spoonful of salt over the beans before lifting the teakettle to pour hot water over them. Then she stretched rubber rings around the necks of the jars and capped them with metal lids. Turning her face away from the steam, she placed the jars into the tub of boiling water.

"Hope I can get a good seal on them when they come out." She wiped sweat from her face with her apron. "At least beans aren't as apt to spoil as corn."

By mid-afternoon, shade from the elm tree didn't help much. Sweat rolled down the back of my neck. Under my dress my legs stuck together. I didn't want to do any more beans. Nancy whined about the flies biting her so I chased her around the house. She wound up in the chicken yard, and I locked the gate behind her. Of course she screamed and howled.

My mother said we were no help and sent us off to the house. Under no circumstances were we to wake Larry who was napping inside. Finding the living room cooler, Nancy and I stretched out on the wood floor in front of the open door, and I guess I went to sleep. I woke up briefly to find my mother on the floor beside us. She didn't stay long. When I got up, she was in the kitchen building the fire again and peeling potatoes for supper.

My mother made another trip to the well. Then she asked me to place water and a washbasin on a bench outside the back door since Frankie and my father would be coming home after their day of threshing. Sure enough, soon there was the roar and rattle of the tractor and wagon coming up the lane. Frankie jumped off the wagon and sent his straw hat sailing to the tree. Already shirtless and brown to the waist, he made short work of his washing up before bounding into the house to ask what there was to eat. My father came up the path mopping his face with a red handkerchief. He took off his shirt to wash and I stared at the whiteness of his shoulders next to the deep tan of his neck and arms. Before entering the kitchen, he buttoned his shirt again and combed his black hair straight back from his sun-reddened forehead. He ruffled Nancy's hair and pulled at my ear. "What you girls been doing to keep out of mischief?"

"We been canning beans." I stretched the last word into a groan.

"Millions of beans," said Nancy.

He took in the jars lined up on the counter. "I'd say zillions of beans."

"There's more to do tomorrow," my mother said.

"Ah, Mom, we just got beans for supper?" asked Frankie.

"There's potatoes and I fried up some side meat." Most people called it bacon. To us, it was side meat, good and fat.

"I'm a meat and potatoes man myself," said my father.

"Meat gets pretty scarce in this house," she returned.

Milk gravy was the last thing my mother fixed before every meal. My father ate it on everything. We all knew the sound of the spoon scraping the iron skillet meant it was time to gather around the big oval table covered with a red and white checkered oilcloth.

"Tom Olson was at the threshing today, wasn't he?" my mother asked. The food had been passed, and everyone concentrated on eating.

"He was there pitching hay," my father said.

"Did he pay you?"

"No, not today."

"It's been two weeks since you did his threshing."

"He'll pay. Times are hard."

Frankie helped himself to more milk from the blue crock. "Tommy says his dad is thinking of buying a new binder."

"What's a binder?" Nancy wanted to know.

"It's a contraption to cut grain, silly. Little girls who get in the way are tied up in shocks of oats and left out in the field with the scarecrows."

"Don't let him kid you, Nan," my father said. "Tom's binder keeps breaking down. Guess he thinks he needs a new one."

"So your pay can wait?"

"He'll get around to it." He shrugged slightly.

I thought of my father, the way I'd seen him working with other men, laughing and swapping stories. I couldn't imagine him asking anyone for money.

"We'll get along," he said.

"Where's the money for extras like shoes for the kids?

I wiggled my bare feet against the chaff and bits of straw that had drifted to the floor from my father and Frankie's overalls. I remembered last winter walking to school across a light skiff of snow. Snow came through a hole in my shoe and soaked my socks. I struck on the idea of cutting pieces from the outhouse catalog to put inside my shoes.

When we finally went to Centerville to buy new shoes, the salesman removed my shoes, and there was all that paper. My mother's face turned red. "I didn't know she had that paper in there." The salesman stared. I was going to catch it, I was sure, but what my mother did was turn to me and ask, "Why didn't you tell me your shoes were that bad?" There were tears in her eyes.

My father broke up a slice of bread into his glass of milk and stirred in some sugar. "Tom'll pay when he can.

Chapter Four

A SATURDAY NIGHT

Come the next Saturday, Mr. Olson still hadn't paid my father for his threshing, something my mother went on about as he drove us into Littleton for our weekly night of trading. It was one of those hot summer nights when women left off their stockings, even for a Saturday night in town. It was a night when everything stuck to your skin—your hair, your clothes. Words stuck too. Like those from Mrs. Olson when my mother met up with her in Perkins' General Store. But by the end of the night, no one was talking about the Olsons.

Nancy and I had waited and waited beside the candy counter in Perkins' Store for my father to come in from his talking and finally gone to complain to our mother who was at the back looking through stacks of yard goods. Holding baby Larry clamped to one hip, she was running her other hand over a flowery blue cotton when Mrs. Olson walked up to her.

"Thinking of making a new dress, Sarah?" Mrs. Olson asked.

"Oh, not really," my mother said shortly, still grumpy about Tom Olson not paying for his threshing.

"We don't see you at church much anymore, Sarah."

"It's a chore with the baby."

"Don't I know it? Didn't I take my young'uns the Sunday after I got up from the birthing bed?"

I remembered when Mrs. Olson brought young Oscar with his squished-up red face to church. Everyone knew he was there, especially the minister who had to talk extra loud over the baby's crying. Now that Oscar was older, he kicked at the seats or crawled under the pews while Tommy swatted him with a paper fan.

Mrs. Olson stood there talking, a piece of sweet corn caught in her teeth. The corn went up and down. "It's nice that Dan still sings in the choir. Suppose he's told you that Susie Grant is playing piano for us. Doing real good too. She plays by ear, don't ya know? Can't imagine anyone having that talent. She really puts some life into the hymn singing."

My mother's face went funny. She used to do the piano playing at church, but not since Larry had been born. My mother could play music that no one else had even heard of. Every month she looked forward to receiving her *Etude* magazine. As soon as the supper dishes were done, she would sit at our black upright piano, open the *Etude* to pages covered with notes, spread her long, thick fingers across the keys, and she'd turn those notes into music.

She dropped the piece of fabric. "Dan'll be waiting. We better be going."

"Oh, I wanted to ask you." Mrs. Olson put her reddened fingers on my mother's arm. "You know we're having a basket dinner at church next Sunday. Some of us thought maybe we should get organized this time so everyone wouldn't be bringing baked beans. I was wondering if you could bring a couple of pies."

The piece of corn was like a yellow flag in the woman's mouth. I knew this time Mrs. Olson had gone too far.

"I'm not much of a pie baker, Blanche," my mother said.

"'Course you are. I remember your ma made wonderful pies."

My mother didn't need to be reminded of that.

Mrs. Olson didn't know when to quit. "Maybe you could bring a fruit cobbler?"

"I don't have fruit on hand just now."

"Well, baked beans then, I guess."

"I don't think we'll be coming this time, Blanche." My mother shifted Larry higher in her arms and headed for the door. I knew we better follow and be quick about it. We got out to the car, but my father was no place in sight.

My mother groaned. "I suppose he's down at the garage showing off that tractor thing he's making. Ruth Ann, go find him. Tell him I'm in the car ready to go."

There were more people on the street than in the stores. I had to dodge knots of women talking about their gardens and how much stuff they had canned. They ignored their kids chasing each other and

running into people. Then there were the high school girls, walking
arm in arm while boys drove their jalopies up and down the street. The
girls talked and laughed extra loud. Maybe it was to get the boys to
notice them. They sure giggled a lot when one of the boys waved or
yelled.

I wanted to cross the street before I got to the beer parlor, but there
were too many men along the curb hanging around their cars, so I was
right in front of the beer place when some man barreled out the door
and jumped into a car. He backed it into the street nearly hitting
another. With a sharp shift of gears, he started again. Someone yelled
at him, "Hey Pete, you forget the Missus?"

The men on the street watched as Pete dodged cars and sped off
down the street. "Think he'll make it home?" one asked.

"Not if the sheriff catches him."

"He'll get home, then."

The men laughed and went into the beer parlor. I crossed the street
to the garage. The smells of grease and gasoline hit me as soon as I
stepped through the wide doors. It looked like all the men who weren't
on the street were inside—leaning against car fenders or sitting on
kitchen chairs some housewife had probably wanted to throw in the
dump. Through the cigarette smoke, it was hard to make out faces. My
mother had said my father always reeked of tobacco when he came
back from the garage.

"Maybe I should take up smoking then you'd be used to it," he had
said.

"Not if you want to live in my house."

At the center of the garage, my father was talking to a group of
men circling the "hoopie" he and Frankie had been working on.
Frankie and his friend Bruce hovered over the contraption like it was
the greatest thing in the world. I had first seen the hoopie when it was
a beat-up car that my father had hitched behind his Case tractor to pull
home from a junkyard.

My mother had looked at the old sedan with rusty fenders and
springs sticking out the cushions. "What you want with that old
thing?"

"I got plans for it."

"Don't suppose those plans call for a polished new body and plush
upholstery—something worth driving to Centerville in?"

"I'd say it's past pleasure rides into town, but it's got one powerful engine, the makings of a real pulling machine."

That's about all it was now—a couple of backless seats behind the long engine riding high on oversized wheels. My father was telling how he had stripped it down, bolted a truck rear axle to the frame, chiseled and sawed off the frame behind the axle. The men hooted when he said he took a draw bar from an old mowing machine and bolted that to the chassis. He ended up by saying, "It's a Buick Master—just what I was looking for. Bound to be a good one."

This kind of talk was pretty boring, but I heard a lot of it when my father was with a group of men. One asked how fast the hoopie would go. Frankie and Bruce shot grins at each other. They spent a lot of time driving the hoopie around open fields, doing all kinds of twists and turns. One time in the barn, I'd heard them talking about how they'd taken it out on the highway—how they'd revved it up to sail over a hill, and there at the bottom was a farmer driving a string of cows across the highway. They laughed about how they had skidded and burned rubber and finally thrown it into reverse to keep from plowing into those cows.

Frankie caught me listening and said he'd skin me alive if I told.

Now I pulled at my father's arm.

"Ruthie, girl, what you doing here?"

"Mom is ready to go home. She had a fight with Mrs. Olson, and she wants to go home quick."

Some of the men seemed to think that was funny. My father grinned a bit. "Guess I'd better be going then."

First, he had to settle with the garage man about when he'd come back for the hoopie. Then Frankie and Bruce wanted to go to the second movie so I had to wait there with those men while my father and Frankie went back and forth about that. Finally my father agreed to drive back into town to pick up the boys after the show.

~ ~ ~

My mother would never have let me ride along with my father to pick up Frankie if she had known what would happen that night. Come to think of it, my father wouldn't have either. Still prickly after her run-in with Mrs. Olson, my mother was tired of me tramping downstairs and complaining it was too hot to sleep. "You might as well go with your dad, since you're keeping Nancy and Larry awake."

It was great being with my father in the truck, windows down, the night alive with songs of crickets and locusts in weedy ditches. I stuck my head out the window, letting cool night air blow through my hair, and wished we could just keep driving. Too soon we were outside the Littleton Theater where Frankie waited. Bruce had gone home with his pa, Frankie told us as he pushed me over to the middle. That way, he got to sit next to the open window, taking up the cool air.

Now that the second show was over, the streets were pretty well empty—only a few stragglers hanging around the beer parlor. As our truck eased along the street, a woman jumped up from the curb and ran to us, waving her arms.

"Dan, thank goodness, it's you." The woman's hair stuck out wildly around her head. Her eyes were wild. "Pete went off and left me here. Could you give me a lift home?"

My father hesitated a little, giving Frankie and me a look. "Sure, Liz, that's right on our way." He motioned for me to climb into the space behind the seats. Frankie had to move away from the window and sit in the middle.

Hunching down in the quilt-cushioned space one of us kids often had to take, I wondered what my mother would think of our giving Liz Patterson a ride. My mother had no use for the Pattersons, especially after my father began to suspect Pete of stealing gasoline from our supply tank. But still Mr. or Mrs. Patterson phoned asking him for help, and still he went. Their place was not on our way. It was down a back road, off by itself.

"This is good of you, Dan. I was afraid I'd have to beg a ride with one of those other guys. None of them was walking too straight."

"So Pete went off and left you, huh?"

"When it comes to drink, he doesn't think about anyone else."

"Drink can do that."

"I should know better than to ride into town with him on a Saturday night, but when else am I going to get off that farm?"

My father didn't say anything, and Frankie stared straight ahead. We rode on like that for a while, windows down and dashboard lights glowing dimly in the truck cab. Mrs. Patterson wore perfume. I wondered if it came from one of those blue bottles of *Evening in Paris* I had seen in Centerville stores.

"Pete's a good guy when he's not drinking," she said.

"Sure, he is." My father nodded. Frankie's chin went up at that. He was probably thinking about Mr. Patterson stealing gas.

I had noticed how women made themselves up for a Saturday night in town, even a place like Littleton. Mrs. Patterson's lipstick was now just a rim around her mouth. She drove her fingers through her hair, then tried to smooth it down. My mother would have said it needed a good combing.

"Pete's a good guy when he's not drinking," Mrs. Patterson said again. She went on about what a good guy Pete was, and my father kept nodding. The warm air and motion of the truck made me sleepy. I stretched out on the quilt.

The truck's sudden stop knocked me against the back of the seat, waking me enough to hear my father's question: "What gun?"

I was completely awake now.

"He gets crazy when he's drinking—thinks I'm running around on him."

"What gun?" he asked again.

"A rifle. He waves it around once in a while."

"Liz, I got my kids with me."

"I know, but I was scared to face him on my own. He'll calm down when he sees you. I just need you to talk to him." She gave a half laugh. "You know Pete. A gunshot would scare him more than anybody."

"Ruth Ann," he said, "you lay down back there and keep out of sight."

The truck crept forward and stopped in the lane that ran across the Pattersons' front yard. My father switched off the headlights. "Frankie, you stay in the truck—and if you need to—drive Ruth Ann home."

My father and Mrs. Patterson closed the truck doors quietly behind them. I stuck my head up to watch them walk to the house, a rundown two-story, nearly hidden by brush and trees. They stepped up on the porch. The screen door banged against the side of the house and there stood Pete framed by the light of the open door. He held a gun.

He pointed it at his wife and yelled, "Git in the house where you belong." He nudged her with the barrel as she went past him.

"Well, howdy, Dan. Nice you come calling. You out to court another woman—even an old bitch like mine? Ain't two women enough for you?"

"Now, Pete, your wife is a fine woman, and no man could take better care of her than you."

"Not the way she tells it. She's always ranting about how she ever got stuck with a bum like me."

"Pete, you need to put that gun away and talk to her gentle like."

"From what I hear, you might have some trouble doing that with your own wife. For me, it'd be simpler and quicker to just gun down all those other men Liz been eyeing."

"There ain't no other men, you know that."

"Oh? Maybe I'm looking at one." Pete raised the gun.

Frankie switched on the headlights.

"Who's out there?" Pete let go a shot, and dirt spun up in front of the headlights.

"Stay down," Frankie hissed and stepped out of the truck.

"Frankie, keep out of this!" my father yelled. Liz appeared in the doorway, but he motioned her away. Then his voice went soft like he was trying to quiet one of our horses. "Pete, I see how upset you are—so upset you're shaking with wanting to protect your wife. I was giving her a lift home like any neighbor would. You'd do the same for my wife."

He glanced back to where Frankie stood beside the truck. "See my son there. You're scaring him. You know my Frankie—he did chores for you that time you were laid up with a broken leg. You don't want to scare him."

Pete lowered his gun. "I remember Frankie. He's a good boy. I don't want to scare him."

"I know that, Pete. You don't want to hurt anyone. You're just upset. Why don't you let me keep the gun until you're feeling better." My father reached for it.

Pete swung the gun away. "I might need it."

"Not tonight, when you're feeling so shaky. You come over to my place after it when you're feeling more yourself." My father's hand was open to him.

Mr. Patterson sounded like he was about to cry. "I don't want to hurt anyone." The gun hung limply from his hand. My father took it from him.

"Pete, you get yourself some rest now. Let Liz rest too so she can fix you some nice breakfast in the morning."

My father held the gun close to his side as he walked back to us. He emptied the gun of shells and laid it down behind the cab.

Neither he nor Frankie said anything until we had gone a ways down the road. "Frank, I told you to stay in the truck."

"Yeah."

Suddenly cold, I wrapped myself in the quilt. We were nearly home when I heard Frankie ask, "What did Pete mean when he said 'two women?'"

"He was drunk. Don't you go bothering your mother about this. I'll tell her what she needs to know."

When we got home, I dashed upstairs without saying anything to my mother. If she knew what had happened, she would never let me go anywhere with my father again. I climbed into bed with Nancy who was fast asleep. She wasn't using the covers, so I pulled them over me. Even with my knees drawn up to my chin, I shivered. My parents talked in the room below me. Her voice burst out. "You could have been killed. The kids! Why didn't you just turn around?"

"What was I supposed to do about Liz?"

"Dump her out. Knowing Liz, she could have managed. Those were our kids you took out there."

Then she was beside my bed. I kept my eyes closed while she smoothed the covers around me. I felt her fingers on my forehead. "You're okay, Ruth Ann. You're home now. You're okay."

Chapter Five

THRESHING DAY

The day began with blood and ended with it. That's the way I remember. Looking back to that day in August, I wonder if it was Decision Day for my mother too.

When my father told her to prepare for threshers coming to our farm, her first reaction was to declare that Peter Patterson better not be among them, because he wasn't eating inside our house. That morning Nancy and I found our mother in the chicken yard ready to swing the axe, and I wondered if she was still thinking about that gun incident. Already a couple of headless chickens were clumps of feathers in a tub. Other chickens, chased down the night before by Frankie, clucked and trod on each other in the small coop.

"You girls up so early? You'll have to stay out of the way." She raised one end of the coop to snatch a chicken by its legs, clamping it tight under one arm, and stretched the chicken's neck between two nails pounded into a tree stump. The bird's eyes bulged in fear, its tongue frozen in its open beak. Nancy whimpered and rocked from one foot to another. Our mother picked up the axe, raised it high and drove it down. Headless, blood spurting, the bird toppled to the ground, somersaulting wing to wing.

"Mommie, Mommie," Nancy screamed, raising her arms in front of her face.

"Take her back to house, Ruth Ann, while I finish these. Get the baby up for me, will you?"

I gave Nancy a push to the house. After the gate was closed safely behind me, I bent my elbows, flapping them chicken style, and danced around Nancy squealing, "Squawk, squawk."

Back at the house, it was the same old thing, feeding Larry and keeping Nancy from teasing him. Even after our mother came in with tubs of plucked chickens, I was stuck watching the little kids.

Finally I heard my grandmother's car coming up the lane and rushed to the screen door. She wore a new apron trimmed with red rickrack over her print dress, and she hurried in with a basket of fresh baked pies and set them on the counter. A little taller than my mother, she had the same brown eyes, but my grandmother's eyes never dropped in shyness the way my mother's did.

"Cherries are coming on good now." My grandmother spread a tea towel over the pies to protect them from flies. "So I made two cherry and two apple pies from what I canned last year."

She looked over at my mother at the sink, her hand plunged into a chicken's body cavity pulling out slippery entrails. "I supposed you would've got that done last night."

Whack, whack went my mother's knife against the cutting board as she chopped off legs and wings. "Dan didn't get the ice until this morning."

My grandmother made a humphing sound.

In his frayed straw hat and clean overalls, my grandfather edged into the kitchen, his back braced against the screen, his chin clamped on boxes he carried.

"You're letting the flies in." My grandmother grabbed a tea towel and flapped it in front of the door.

"Did you want me to leave these things on the stoop?" He eased the boxes onto the table.

"Careful, there are dishes in that one."

Without a word, he pushed through the screen again and returned with a large pot of homemade noodles and beef. Then he was gone. The screen door swished shut behind him like a sigh of relief as he escaped to the fields and men's work.

My grandmother eyed the crumbs and sticky smudges on the oil-clothed table. "Let's give this a good scrub down, Ruth Ann, before I unpack my dishes."

I brought her a greasy, dripping dishrag. She dangled it between her thumb and forefinger like it was something dead. Dropping it in the sink, she said, "I think I brought some clean ones."

My mother chopped more legs and wings.

The evening before, she had put extra leaves in the kitchen table and told Frankie to bring in the washhouse table to butt up against it. After my grandmother had cleaned and cleaned the kitchen table, I helped her remove newspaper packing from her water glasses and set them out. "I brought plenty of glasses. Can't have you using tin cans like Edith Crandall did that time."

My mother's head jerked up, her eyes hard as buttons. "We haven't sunk that low."

"Just knew you needed extry was all I meant. I brought a tablecloth too."

Things picked up a lot when my grandmother was around. She had me help her scrub the washhouse table before smoothing her bright, flowery tablecloth across stains of soap and lye. Next, I was set to work shelling peas out on the back stoop. It was nice to be outside the kitchen, the light breeze tickling my forehead and neck. In the distance across the barn lot, shocks of grain stood in the oat field like straw children. A man walked beside a horse-drawn hayrack, forking the shocks and pitching them to another man on the rack who built the load, bundle upon bundle. They would be fed to the machine that flashed in the sun like an armored monster. By evening the straw children would be gone.

On this side of the screen door I could listen without having to see the tired set of my mother's mouth, the slump of her shoulders.

"I supposed some of the neighbors would bring food in," my grandmother said.

"Trudy Benz dropped off a cake, but said she couldn't stay."

"What about Blanche Olson?"

"Not likely. Not since I turned down her basket dinner invitation."

"You really ought to go to church. Play the piano for them again."

"It's not worth the hassle of getting everyone ready. Don't think anyone misses me much. Like Blanche says, 'They have Susie Grant playing piano by ear.'"

"Suppose Dan goes."

"Usually. They're always after him to sing in the choir. He takes the girls. Frankie isn't interested."

"Is that woman still in the choir?" my grandmother asked.

"I suppose she is. I don't keep track of her."

"Maybe you should."

"Don't start." There was the loud clank of the stove lid. I guessed my mother was checking the fire. Her voice came through the screen door. "Ruth Ann, I need more cobs."

"Ah, Mom." Just when it was getting interesting. I no sooner got back from the barn with the cobs than I was told to round up every available chair. My grandmother helped Nancy and me carry the piano bench and place it at one end of the table. My mother found a board in the washhouse, and we laid that across two chairs to make another place.

"Frankie and maybe Jerry can sit there," she said.

The smells of bread fresh from the oven and fried chicken sputtering on the wood range filled the hot, steamy kitchen. My grandmother had me run back and forth to the table with plates of thick, juicy red sliced tomatoes, bowls of leaf lettuce, wilted in a warm vinegar and sugar dressing while she and my mother mashed potatoes, stirred gravy, and hovered over bubbling pots of fresh peas, creamed corn, and green beans cooked with onions and a slab of bacon.

The Seth Thomas clock struck twelve when I heard the first tractor pull into the lane, followed by teams of horses heading for the watering trough. Soon men in overalls, talking and milling around, filled the yard, and a heavy man pulled his shirt up to show a track of brown hair running down his front. He jerked the rough strip of huck toweling from its nail on a tree and brushed at seeds and chaff caught in his belly button.

"Hey, Art, you're supposed to leave that stuff in the field," someone called out.

"He's trying to start a new crop," another said.

One man poured water over his bald head.

"That's okay, Fred," said my father. "We've got more water out yonder in the well."

I spotted Jerry from the next farm in the crowd and ran outside. Maybe we could play something later. He didn't even say, "Hi." He just moved off to stand next to Frankie and the new kid Bruce. My mother had ragged Frankie about running around with Bruce so much. She said he was an accident waiting to happen.

Brushing her hair back and straightening her apron, my mother called through the screen that dinner was ready.

My father held open the door. "Make yourself at home."

With hats in hand, the men entered the house one by one. Suddenly quiet, they stopped their talk except to nod. "Howdy, Miz Moreton.

Good day, Miz Hinrichson." They could have been bashful little kids, the way they edged around each other to find places at the table. My mother gave Mr. Olson the once over as he sidled into the last place.

I had never seen so many men inside our house. The threshers looked smaller without their hats—a little naked with their white foreheads and mashed down hair. Saturday nights when the Clark brothers were out on the street, I thought Matt was handsome. Now I saw he was bald. It was easy to pick out Bruce's father, Hank Benz. Barrel shaped and puffed-up important, he was loud in his bragging about his new tractor and how many loads had been threshed at his farm the week before.

"Yeah," my father laughed. "'Course he's not telling you that newfangled tractor is so green and loud that two teams of horses ran off in protest, and we had to stop everything to chase them down."

The threshers did not hold back once the food was passed. My mother and grandmother fairly ran with refills on coffee or lemonade, more potatoes, more bread, another platter of chicken, then pie and cake. They kept me running too, so I couldn't pay much attention to the talk. The Clark brothers, who my father had said once managed to be on every crew that came along because they needed a free meal, went on about threshing runs they'd been on. Mr. Benz's voice drowned them out, saying he had followed crews from Texas to Montana. "I never seen a loader I couldn't beat."

Jerry, just a kid like me, was acting awfully stuck up in spite of being squeezed in at the table by all those big men. He was as bad as Frankie, wide-eyed and leaning in close, trying to catch every word Bruce said about his new jalopy. I suppose it was something like our hoopie. I wondered how Frankie felt about Bruce boasting about how his jalopy would make our hoopie eat dust.

Finally the men pushed back their chairs and rose from the table. "Mighty good eats," they said nodding to my mother and grandmother. "Best pie I ever 'et," said one, patting his belly. Hank Benz actually belched as he and others trooped outside to flop down in the shade of the elm tree.

Bored with the sight of snoozing, open-mouthed men, I was about to turn from the door when Bruce motioned to Frankie. They looked around and took off to Bruce's jalopy. Soon the coughing grind of its engine rumbled across the yard.

The open jalopy sped, backfiring, down the lane. A couple of men woke up long enough to grin at each other and rolled over for more sleep. My mother was suddenly at my side. The jalopy braked sharply at the end of the lane, squealing tires and spinning up dirt as it turned onto the gravel road. I had ridden with the boys a time or two—times my mother didn't know about—and I almost felt that burst of speed as Bruce gunned the engine, the boys' laughter rising above the dust rolling out behind them. My mother stepped out as Mr. Benz slapped his thigh. "That boy! The only speed he knows is wide open."

My father returned her look. "They'll be back in a bit."

Her eyes followed the dust cloud until it dropped behind the next hill. She drew back inside and cleared the table. The men returned to work.

Mid-afternoon, Jerry appeared at the kitchen door, like a big kid saddled with a little kid's job. "Frankie is helping Bruce pick up a load of bundles. My dad thought you might need some help getting eats out to the field."

"That's mighty kind, Jerry," said my mother. "You and Ruth Ann can handle that job fine. Ruth Ann, you'll need shoes."

She packed Frankie's old coaster wagon with jugs of lemonade and a pot of coffee. "Homemade bread spread with butter and a dollop of apple butter is all I've got." She placed paper sacks in the wagon. "Most wives probably send out sandwiches of store-bought bread and baloney."

"It's a good plenty, Sarah. Besides, I'd take your bread anytime," my grandmother said, adding a bag of cookies.

With Jerry pulling and me steadying the jugs of lemonade, we bumped along through the barn lot and up across the pasture to the oat field. The pulling got hard as we climbed the hill, and Jerry kept switching hands.

"Let me pull," I said.

He reared back his shoulders. "I can do it."

We came onto the stubbly oat field where everything—the very air and the ground under my feet—seemed to vibrate with the grinding, whirring, and roaring of the tractor and threshing machine. Horses tossed their heads as drivers slapped reins to line them up on either side of the thresher, while men stood high on hayracks and pitched bundles of oats into the head of the machine. Somewhere in that noise, the thresher's steel teeth took the bundles in and slashed the cords. The thresher shook and rumbled deep in its belly and coughed out seeds, carrying them up a clanking shaft and spitting them into a waiting wagon.

My father stood atop the thresher with his legs planted wide like he was one with its gears and moving belts. He lifted his hat briefly and ran his fingers back through his thick black hair. Crooking his arm to shade his eyes against the sun, he looked over the men working to the beat of the machines. In a little while, he spotted me and Jerry with our wagon of snacks and gave my grandfather the signal to shut off the tractor.

Their chins dripping sweat, men surrounded our coaster wagon to gulp down great cups of lemonade or coffee. They snaked grimy hands into sacks to pull out one sandwich after another. Frankie and Bruce were first in line for the cookies. Jerry and I grinned behind their backs, thinking of the cookies we had stashed in our pockets.

It was a good thing because in no time only crumbs were left. My father was back cranking up the Case tractor, while my grandfather waited on the seat. Soon the coughing, sputtering, and grinding gears of the thresher settled into a rhythmic roar. The ground shook again. Frankie was slugging down the last of the lemonade when Bruce sidled up to him. "Hey, our hay rack's ready. How about us being first in line and first to unload?"

Frankie didn't seem too keen about the idea, but he couldn't let on because the Clark brothers were close by listening. "Unloading ain't kid stuff," said the bald one. "Your pa gonna let you do that?"

Bruce's chin went up. "I've done it before."

"Sure you have." The brothers laughed and started off to their rack.

Jerry's father had overheard too. "Hadn't you better let your dad take it through?"

"I've done it before," repeated Bruce. "Besides, Pa has his own rack to unload."

"I'd feel better if you checked with your dad." Jerry's father shook his head and went to man the seed wagon.

Frankie edged up to Bruce. "Have you really unloaded before?"

"Naw, but I've watched plenty of times." At the sound of my grandfather revving up the Case tractor, Bruce was at a run, yelling back at Frankie. "Come on, maybe we can beat my old man."

My father walked from tractor to thresher, checking the belt that powered the thresher.

"Dad's gonna be mad," I said.

Frankie flung me a dirty look and ran to catch Bruce. Jerry and I watched them climb aboard the rack, stepping from bundle to bundle, like they were walking on rubber balls. Bruce took the reins. He urged the horses forward, trying to pull their load along one side of the feeder. With his hired man driving his new tractor, Mr. Benz stood atop his rack. They pulled up on the other side. Bruce's father called out something, but in all the noise I couldn't make out his words.

With a know-it-all grin, Jerry said, "Bruce can't handle the team." The horses fought against their reins, shy and tack, angling the rack away from the thresher. Bruce slapped the reins to move the team in closer, but they balked again.

"They're afraid of the noise and belts," Jerry said, still being the know-it-all.

By now the Clark brothers had pulled into line behind Bruce. Maybe that told Bruce they had to unload fast. He motioned Frankie to take charge of the horses, grabbed a pitchfork, and climbed higher on the wobbly bundles.

"He's too far from the machine," Jerry said. He wasn't being a show-off now.

Bruce swung his head from the Clark brothers crowding in behind him to Mr. Benz standing astride his load, like he was waiting for Bruce to do something. Bruce drove his pitchfork into a bundle and pitched to the feeder. Then another and another. Mr. Benz turned to his own load and matched Bruce pitch for pitch, like it was a race. The Clark brothers, suddenly in no hurry, pulled back on their horses.

My father stood atop the thresher now, his eyes on Bruce, then Hank Benz. From the grimace on my father's face, I knew Frankie was in for it. Mr. Benz stopped for a minute to watch his son move to the back of his load where the rack was farthest from the machine. Bruce gave a glance to his father then forked a bundle. With an extra swing of his body, he pitched the bundle to the feeder. In that instant, his legs shot apart, as if the shocks had shifted under his feet. Still gripping the pitchfork, Bruce flung both arms out for balance. I got the crazy idea he was trying to catch the bundle, the way his body followed the same path to the feeder. He fell on the moving conveyer belt and just lay there.

Frantically pitching bundles out of his way to reach Bruce, Mr. Benz' mouth was a black hole. Frankie's horses tossed their heads, trying to move backward. My father ran to the front of the thresher, shouting and motioning to my grandfather to turn off the tractor. It sputtered and died, but the belt kept moving. My father jumped to the ground, grabbed a crowbar, jammed it into the gears, then threw his weight against the belt. It seemed forever before the conveyer creaked to a halt. Bruce lay on the conveyer hunched up like another bundle of oats.

"Why doesn't he get up?" I asked.

Jerry didn't answer. Everything had stopped, the machines, the men atop the wagons—frozen against the sky like a jammed film at an afternoon picture show. Then as if his legs and arms hurt, Mr. Benz bent over the feeder and lifted his son. The pitchfork came up with him. It had become a bloody part of Bruce's body.

Silence ballooned over stilled machines, yet it beat in my head as loud as drums. Something moved in front of me, blocking the scene. An arm circled my shoulders and turned me away. I heard Jerry's father's voice. "Son, take Ruth Ann home. Tell her ma to call someone for help. No, leave the wagon. Go. Hurry."

Jerry grabbed my hand and pulled me across the field. My feet wouldn't work right. They slipped on uneven ground, stumbled over clods, clumped grass. Behind me, the balloon of silence burst, pierced by screams. I knew it was Mr. Benz. I fell. Sharp stubble cut into my hands, my knees. Jerry jerked at my arm. I was running again, running from the sound of Mr. Benz.

My mother and grandmother appeared, their skirts flying as they rushed to meet us. My mother grabbed me, but she shouted at Jerry, "Frankie? Is Frankie…?

"No, no," Jerry choked. "No, you gotta call someone."

"I'll call." My grandmother twisted around and ran back into the house.

My mother gripped my shoulders. "You all right, Ruth Ann?" I nodded and I was alone as she ran to the field.

My grandmother came out of the house and wrapped her arms around both Jerry and me, pulling us close to her strong body. We waited like that until a horse-drawn wagon creaked down the hill to us. Men walked wordlessly and separately on either side of the wagon. To the end of the line my mother walked with Frankie, her arm tight around his shoulders.

Chapter Six

THE FUNERAL

The Holbrook place—that's what everyone called it even though the Benz family had bought it over a year before—was set back off the road behind a stand of elm trees. I had once heard my mother say she'd love to have that big two-story house with its encircling porch. But she had protested coming here on this day. "Why should we all go crowding in on Mr. and Mrs. Benz? I'd think they'd want to be left alone."

"It's expected," my father said.

Other people must have felt the same way. Cars were parked along the lane, and men stood in little knots on the grassy yard like they didn't want to go any farther. Their eyes slid over us as I followed my mother, father, and Frankie along the narrow sidewalk to the house. Some of the men lifted their heads to nod to my father, but none of them approached us.

The whole day had been strange. At the church people had acted nothing like they did on ordinary Sundays when they came in talking and talking over Susie Grant's pounding away on the piano prelude. When my mother had held the job of pianist, she said she wondered why she bothered since no one listened. This day people were all stiff and buttoned into dark clothes. My mother shushed me when my patent leather shoes clicked on the wood floor.

I tried to sit still in the pew, but my feet dangled above the floor and the hard wood cut into the back of my legs. Across the aisle Jerry was hunkered down between his parents. His shoulders twitched under a suit coat I'd never seen him wear. It pleased me a little to know he had a hard time sitting still too.

The only one allowed to talk was the minister. His voice, low like he had a cold, went on and on. I guess it was catching, because pretty soon the church was filled with sniffing sounds. Handkerchiefs fluttered in women's hands all around me. I thought maybe I should be crying too, but my mother sat rigid and dry-eyed, as did my father.

Finally the minister was done talking, and we could leave the church. People slumped out without speaking to one another. It was like someone made a rule against talking and laughing. Hands went over faces to cover any coughing or clearing of throats. We remained quiet as our car followed in the line moving to the cemetery.

The cemetery seemed different too. I'd been there before with my grandparents when we put flowers on graves of people I had never heard of. Concentrating on not walking on the graves of dead people, I hadn't noticed then how black the cemetery gates and fence looked.

Inside the gates, there were only the sounds of car doors closing, the shuffling of feet along the gravel path. I dragged along behind my parents and Frankie, studying the gravestones. Older stones stood like gray old men, their names worn away. There was a tiny square stone with a lamb engraved on it. I was trying to figure out why a lamb would be in the graveyard when Tommy Olson and Jerry popped out at me from behind the taller stones. Jerry's father quickly stepped off the path and brought his son back in line, but Tommy had ducked out of sight. Jerry grinned at me and threw a glance over his shoulder. I looked back, and Tommy was balancing on first one stone then another.

My mother grabbed my hand and held it tightly as we edged in close to the family at the grave. My father stood near the front because he had been asked to sing. "Beyond the sunset, O blissful morning when with our Savior heav'n is begun…." I had heard him sing the song at church many times, but I had never heard his voice like that, all gravelly and sad. "Beyond the sunset, O glad reunion with our dear loved ones who've gone before…." Is that what the song meant? I wished I had stayed home with Nancy. I didn't want to be here with these grown-ups, dabbing at their eyes.

In pictures of funerals, I had never seen the faces. They were hidden as people huddled under umbrellas, shiny black with rain. But in this place gated away from fields and road, it wasn't raining. I looked away from the hole cut into the earth, where grass bent under the weight of freshly dug black soil, to the pine trees that rose straight and green to a string of puffy clouds in a blue sky. It was like a picture book. Like a normal day.

I buried my face in the folds of my mother's dress and tried not to hear the moans coming from Bruce's mother. I felt my mother's hand on my hair. Finally we were moving again in another silent line to the cars. And in no time at all we were at the Benz place. Approaching the porch, my mother whispered to my father, "Let's not stay long. Just pay our respects." A couple of men were sitting on a swing at the far end of the porch, and they watched us mount the steps. I had seen them that day at the threshing. They did not speak.

"Sarah, Dan, do come in. The Benz' will be so glad you came." Mrs. Olson held the door open for us. She was dressed in that outfit she wore to church, the blue dress with tiny flowers blending in with the spots on it. Red cherries on her white straw hat spilled over the brim to her sharp nose.

"Such a terrible thing," she said in her high voice. "So sad."

She didn't seem very sad. Beneath those cherries, her eyes swung over me and Frankie and darted back to my mother. "And you brought the children."

"We thought they should be here," said my father. He had said maybe it would help Frankie if I came. I didn't know how. Frankie wouldn't even look at me. The way he kept his head down, I didn't see how he could look at anyone.

And I was afraid to look at him. Afraid his eyes would be all red-rimmed from the crying I had heard during the night. My big brother Frankie—I couldn't believe those sounds were coming from him. But they went on and on until the stairs creaked under my mother's footsteps. At last, they faded under the soft strokes of her voice.

Mrs. Olson wasn't shy about looking at Frankie. "He was about your age, wasn't he?"

I supposed Mrs. Olson knew Frankie was on the hayrack with Bruce. Frankie shrank deeper into the suit jacket my mother had insisted he wear.

"Yes, Ma'am." His voice sounded like his tie had cut off all his air.

"Bruce was a year or two older," my father spoke up. "It was a terrible accident."

Neither of my parents seemed too eager to step into the living room. It was one of those "don't-touch-anything" rooms, filled with family photographs, knick-knacks, and furniture you didn't want to sit

on. Some people I had seen at the church sat on the edges of
upholstered chairs and sofas as if it would be wrong to lean against the
tasseled throws and fancy cushions. A farm couple bent to shake hands
with the man and woman who sat on a settee. The woman wiped her
eyes with a scrunched-up handkerchief. I wondered if the big,
shapeless man next to her could be Mr. Benz. He didn't seem anything
close to the bear-like man from threshing day.

"They're taking it so hard," Mrs. Olson said. "But it was a
beautiful service, wasn't it? Just beautiful. And he looked so nice."

Frankie's eyes jerked to Mrs. Olson's face. I sucked in my breath,
afraid he would tell the woman she was crazy. I had tried not to see
into the casket, but I had to walk right by it to get into the church.
What lay inside didn't look anything like Bruce, the boy who laughed
and joked with Frankie.

"Of course, we're in such shock," Mrs. Olson said. The cherries
bounced ever so slightly and her voice changed, making me think of
those church potlucks she organized when a visiting preacher came to
town. "Everyone brought so much food. It's set out all lovely with
some of the flowers in the dining room. I know Mrs. Benz would want
you to help yourselves. Oh, here come the Thompsons."

I didn't know what to do when my family moved to Mr. and Mrs.
Benz. I sure didn't want to see the Benzes cry. I pulled away from my
mother and wandered into the dining room.

Like Mrs. Olson said, there was lots of food, sandwiches, potato
salad, and all kinds of cakes and pies. Jerry was there looking hungry
while his mother served lemonade for people coming through. She
glanced up and smiled—one of those half smiles when you know
you're not supposed to appear happy. "Jerry, why don't you and Ruth
Ann fix up some plates and go on out to the porch? I'll tell Ruth Ann's
mother where she is."

Carrying lemonade and plates topped with large chunks of
chocolate cake, Jerry and I squeezed out the screen door past Mrs.
Olson's glare and plopped down at the far end of the porch.

The two men who had been at the threshing still sat on the swing at
the other end of the porch. I was biting into the wedge of cake,
ignoring the chocolate crumbs that fell onto my good dress, when I
heard my father's name.

"Dan's boy is taking this kinda hard, ain't he?"

"Well, he was on the rack with the Benz boy."

"You suppose Dan could have stopped it?"

"Hank Benz was right there, and he didn't stop it. Dan probably thought the kid could handle it since his pa didn't say nothing. Not for Dan to tell him what to do."

Jerry punched me. "How about getting some more cake?"

"You can have mine." I shoved the cake away from me.

The cake didn't last long. Jerry flicked crumbs away from his mouth with the back of his hand. "Why don't we go down to the crick after we get home?"

"Mom'd never let me."

"Your ma's all worked up about this, same as mine. They'll never notice."

"I guess." I brushed at a piece of chocolate on my skirt. It left a dark smear. My mother would not like that.

"At least the rain has held off," said one of the men on the swing.

"Maybe we can get back in the field tomorrow."

"You think Dan'll be ready?"

"If it don't rain, he'll be ready."

Chapter Seven

JAMBOREE

The funeral was scary because everyone was different, walking and talking like people I didn't know. For a while after Bruce got killed, grown-ups kept on their long faces, their voices husky when speaking of the dare-devil boy they had once chided for tearing down gravel roads on his jalopy. But Jamboree days were coming, and soon voices lifted. "Life has to go on."

The Littleton Jamboree was a once-a-year good time that no one wanted to miss. The parade had always been a big thing for me, but this year it had left me with an uneasy, sickish feeling. The day started off wrong with my brother Frankie announcing he wasn't going. My mother said she didn't feel much like going into town either. She'd been like this since that awful threshing day, showing no interest in church or what she called gossipy Saturday nights in Littleton. I guessed it was because of what happened to Bruce, although I never heard her talk about it, except for the one time she fired off words at my father saying it could've been our Frankie killed on that machine.

I wasn't about to let the accident keep me from the Jamboree. It took some concentrated coaxing to convince my father to give me a ride into town and let me stay overnight at Aunt Sophie's house.

We arrived in time for my father to drop me off on Main Street for the parade. Squeezing in front of other onlookers, I found myself within waving distance of Jerry. He was with some other boys and didn't seem glad to see me. I decided I didn't care and turned to the school band, picturing myself as one of those short-skirted girls leading the parade, stepping high and punching out the rhythm with batons. From Jerry and his friends' giggling and taunts, I gathered they liked the girls too. Neighbors partially disguised in attic-aged costumes rode by on makeshift floats decked out with crumpled crepe paper. We cheered them all.

Another float went by and for me everything changed. It was a simple hayrack with two men atop a load of hay. The scene whirled, and I saw only one person with something red blossoming from the pitchfork in his hand. The glitz from the parade was gone, the music stilled. The cheering echoed a different sound. I was back in that threshing field again, Jerry beside me sucking in his breath, not believing what fell into the jaws of the threshing machine. Men stood motionless atop hay wagons. The very air of the field went blank. The roar of tractor and thresher choked off. The beat of silence drummed in my head. That was before the screaming began.

The picture went wavery until my eyes found Jerry again. For an instant I knew we were in the same place. Another float carrying the baseball team came along, and Jerry cheered again. The two men atop the hay wagon were not carrying pitchforks but guitars. What I had seen as blotches of blood were simply handkerchiefs sprouting from their overall pockets. With the sounds of carnival and more floats going by, the image faded, and by suppertime at my aunt's house, it was scarcely a memory.

Aunt Sophie, Uncle Josh, and my cousin Mikey lived a block off Main Street. I couldn't believe my mother was going to let me stay overnight at their house while the Jamboree was on. But her attention was on Frankie now.

It was hard for me to think of Aunt Sophie as my father's sister. With her white hair, she looked too old, and she never laughed. After supper at her house that evening, Aunt Sophie had said she had some things to do for her church meeting the next day and wouldn't it be nice if Mikey—of course, she called him Michael—took me to the Jamboree. Mikey agreed. He was always the perfect child when his mother was around. Aunt Sophie didn't know much about boys—how they didn't like being bothered with kids younger than them, especially girls.

Mikey and I heard music as soon as we left the house. By night, the Jamboree changed Littleton's Main Street to a whole different place, alive with colored lights and swirling sound. Mikey ran ahead, dashing from one sight to another. I stood with my mouth open, wanting to take in this make-believe street before it disappeared.

There was the music of the merry-go-round with its horses painted pink and orange, colors that horses could never be. My heart beat in the same rhythm as the horses moved up and down.

Mikey yanked at my arm. "Come on."

"Aren't we going to ride on the merry-go-round?"

"Like some little kid?" Insulted, he rushed on ahead.

I started to follow but the cotton candy booth sidetracked me. Outside the booth, a little girl with her mother watched the candy maker dip a paper cone into a big kettle holding some kind of bubbling mixture. The candy maker twirled the cone in the pot, gathering a pink cottony cloud. The little girl stood on tiptoe, her eyes wide as the fluffy cloud grew. With a final swing of the cone, the candy maker cut off a tail stringing down to the kettle and handed the cotton candy to the waiting child.

I fingered the single coin in my dress pocket. I could almost taste the sugary candy dissolving in my mouth. I gripped the coin and moved on to a food booth displaying pies with mile-high meringue, cakes with inch-thick chocolate frosting, canned pickles, peaches, and loaves of bread. Women in short-sleeved print dresses leaned in close, pointing at ribbons attached to the food. "Well, I never," said one, "a blue ribbon on Mrs. Jacobs' bread."

"I'll bet it's hollow in the center," said her friend.

I pushed between two women to see cookies cut in different shapes. One of the women gave me a dirty look. "It's one of those ragtag Moreton kids."

The other nodded. "What more could you expect? You heard about that boy getting killed out at their place, didn't you?"

I wanted out of there, fast! A big woman got in my way. It was an accident that I knocked the chocolate pie out her hands. The pie spilled over her shoes. The tin bounced and spun down the street, flinging out a chocolate trail. With a leap over the goopy mess, I took off in the opposite direction.

I couldn't wait to tell Mikey about the woman with chocolate feet. Where was he? Hundreds of people moved with the swirl of sound, the merry-go-round, up and down and around, a gong clanging at the top of a pole, onlookers cheering for the man to swing the sledge hammer one more time. A line of laughing, arm-linked high schoolers plowed into me as they snaked their way through the crowd. They didn't break their hold on each other, just yelled, "Watch yourself, kid."

Mikey wasn't in the cluster of kids digging into large sacks of popcorn at the popcorn stand. He wasn't at the hotdog stand either— just a bunch of men stuffing their faces. I fingered that coin in my pocket again.

Then I saw my cousin standing near the Ferris wheel, yelling and waving back at some boys leaning over their seats at the top.

"Where you been?" he asked me. "I'm going on the next ride."

The wheel of lights circled even higher than Mr. Perkins' store. How wonderful to be up so high and look down on everything. "Can I come with you?"

"You got money?"

"Sure." I pulled out my single coin.

Finally the Ferris wheel stopped and the attendant steadied a seat for us. My legs felt trembly when he latched the bar. We started up. The seat swung. We stopped several more times to let riders on. The seat swung with each stop. Higher and higher we went, over all those people enviously looking up at us, over the merry-go-round whirling and whirling, over street lights spinning off in every direction, above the trees, above Mr. Perkins' store, above the flat, dark tops of other stores and the peaked roof of the movie house.

At the highest point, we jerked to another stop. Mikey laughed and rocked the seat. I gripped the bar. It didn't help. Mikey leaned over the side waving to people below. I thought Jerry was among the watchers, but as the seat rocked more, I was too intent on hanging on to be sure. With a jerk we were moving again, starting to drop. This was not like scooping the hills in my father's truck. This was worse than Frankie punching me in the stomach. It was wanting to throw up after eating green apples. I was going to be sick. We climbed again, faster than before, over the merry-go-round whirling, lights spinning, bells clanging. Then we were dropping again. Up again, faster. I closed my eyes, not caring about being above Mr. Perkins' store or the movie theatre. Dropping again the seat rocking, Mikey laughing, up again dropping. Finally we slowed. The man lifted the bar. We were on the ground, and I tried to walk.

"Hey, scaredy cat." It was Jerry, calling out to me. "What's a matter?"

Things were still going round and round. Dismissing Jerry with what I hoped was a dirty look, I hurried to follow my cousin who seemed to give no thought to leaving me behind. Still unsteady on my feet, I caught up near the town park where carnival music came from a tent. Inside, a girl balanced herself on the back of a white horse. I couldn't believe how she stood there on tiptoe and didn't fall. The girl was pretty, dressed in a gold and purple sparkly costume flaring over blue tights. Blond curls piled atop her head, like she was a fancy doll. Around and around she rode to the music, the horse stepping in time.

The carnival music sounded tinny compared to the sounds of drums and all kinds of horns coming from the bandstand at the center of the park. Mikey and I were crossing the grass to listen when some kind of ruckus bellowed from a travel trailer parked behind the carnival tent. That noise was much more interesting than the band, and we headed to it. At first, I was a little scared, thinking probably some strange carnival people were fighting inside the trailer, but the commotion came from a group of boys behind it, shouting, "Give it to him."

"Stay here." Mikey motioned me to stop.

I stuck right by his side, and we edged our way into the group. At the center of a barren patch of ground, some kid with yellow, broom-like hair fought another kid. The other kid was Frankie. It was crazy the way they swung at one another. It couldn't be real because in the background there was band music, high trumpet and low trombone. It was like a fight in a Tom Mix movie, the guy in a black hat punching a guy in a white hat, except there were no hats. That was my brother hitting and being hit and yelling, "Take it back. Take it back."

The broom-haired kid grabbed Frankie's shirt and spun him around. Frankie fell in the dirt. He was up again, swinging. The awful sound of fist hitting bone.

"Wow, right in the kisser," someone yelled. Jerry had edged into the group, but he did not join in the yelling.

A splotch of blood grew over the other kid's face. In the park, people sat on the grass, listening to the roll of drums and the crash of cymbals. The blood scared me. Maybe it scared Frankie too. He backed off, turned and walked away. Around the bandstand there was applause. The boys egging on the fight went quiet. Their feet made scuff marks in the dirt like they didn't know whether to go or stay. Jerry was the first to leave, without saying anything to me. One by one, the other boys slouched off in different directions, leaving behind the broom-haired kid with the bloody nose.

Mikey and I caught up with Frankie. "What you kids doing here?" he asked.

"You got him good," Mikey said.

"You think so? Well, maybe he won't be blaming me or my dad for the accident anymore." He brushed dirt off his shirt.

His shirt was torn. "Mom'll raise Cain," I said.

"Don'cha go telling. Go on back to Aunt Sophie's."

"How're you getting home?" I asked.

"Same way I got here. Walk."

The girl who rode the white horse came through a flap at the back of the tent. Up close, she looked older, and her costume was worn, some of the sparkly beads missing. Barely glancing at us, she lit a cigarette before turning to the travel trailer. As she mounted the steps to the door, I noticed a large hole descending in a run down her tights.

~ ~ ~

As soon as Mikey and I got to Aunt Sophie's house, she declared it was past our bedtime. We'd have to get up early, she said, to get to tomorrow's church meeting on time. After all, she and Uncle Josh would be doing the preaching.

It felt good to escape to the tiny bedroom off Aunt Sophie's kitchen, to change into my nightgown and climb into bed. But I couldn't escape the sounds of the carnival coming through the open window, or the steady stream of boys yelling from cars as they raced past the house and the screech of brakes as they rounded the next corner. I wondered where Frankie was.

My sleep got mixed up with the colored lights, music pumping up and down. Then I was falling. No, boys around Frankie were hitting and yelling. "Ruth Ann, Ruth Ann, it's time to get up." It was Aunt Sophie at the bedroom door calling me for morning devotions. At home I got up for breakfast, but at Aunt Sophie's this thing called "devotions" came first.

In the living room, Uncle Josh waited on a straight back chair, his broad fingers tapping the Bible spread across his knees. Aunt Sophie pulled up chairs for herself and me. Sitting beside his father, Mikey ignored me, his eyes on the Bible in his hands. First Uncle Josh turned into Uncle Joshua and read like an actor in a play. Then Aunt Sophie became Aunt Sophia and did her reading. Then Mikey. I kept my head down and took a deep breath when they passed me by. All the reading seemed to be about bloody battles where God struck down sinners. One story that bothered me was about some woman who turned into a pillar of salt just because she looked back.

My legs were good and stiff from hanging over a chair so high my feet wouldn't touch the floor. "Ruth Ann, it's time to kneel before our Lord," Aunt Sophie said. "I don't suppose your mother ever taught you about that."

I could have told her that my father never said anything about kneeling either. He liked singing in church choirs, but saying a quick grace before meals was about as religious as he got. And he was Aunt Sophie's brother?

The wood floor was hard against my knees. I tucked my nightgown under them, but it didn't help much. With some loud groans, Uncle Josh managed to get his bulky body into a kneeling position. He became Uncle Joshua again, booming out words as though God was out in the back yard hiding behind the car shed. Aunt Sophia took up the prayer, her voice rolling, rising, and falling. The second time she came to the phrase, "Oh Lord, we just pray," I shifted, ready to get to my feet, but my aunt was only getting started. Every time the words, "Oh Lord, we just pray," came around, the floor got harder.

Finally devotions were over, and we had to rush through breakfast and hurry to dress for the church meeting. When I appeared before my aunt in the same dress I had worn to the Jamboree, she was not happy.

"Didn't your mother send along something more suitable for you to wear to church? That dress is much too short. And where are your stockings?"

Probably my mother didn't think going to church was any big thing. And stockings? It was summertime.

I tagged along behind Mikey, Uncle Josh, and Aunt Sophie to the car, a big used Packard that Uncle Josh had purchased from the town's undertaker the year before. Uncle Josh turned to Mikey. "Son, it's 'bout time you was doing some driving."

My aunt gasped. "Oh no, Joshua. You can't mean that."

"I said it, didn't I?" Uncle Josh flipped the keys to Mikey who was not even thirteen yet.

Mikey looked at the car, all polished up, ebony black gleaming in the summer sunshine. I thought maybe he was a tad scared the way he shifted his shoulders, but he put on his best face. "You bet, Pa."

Aunt Sophie let out a breathless, "Oh Lord, I just pray." Her Bible in hand, she stepped up on the car's running board and seated herself on the back seat. There was nothing for me to do but climb in beside her.

Heavy car doors banged shut enclosing us in stale, warm air. We hastily rolled the windows down, but dust from the upholstered seats made me want to sneeze. Sitting straight as a preacher with her arms folded in front of her, my aunt became Aunt Sophia again. I knew that under her long-sleeved jacket she wore a soft white blouse with a lace stand-up collar. Something like a queen might wear, the collar seemed to support her head crowned with glittering combs tucked in her heavy coils of hair.

My cousin had driven his father's farm jalopy several times, but that had been out in the open field where there were no yellow lines or curbs to contend with. With a grinding of gears and some jumps and jerks, Mikey got the Packard out of the driveway.

"Josh-u-aa?" came from my aunt.

"Woman, he's got to learn some time."

Mikey drove down a side street since the carnival was closing down on Main. We passed the gas station at the edge of town and turned onto the highway. Aunt Sophia opened her Bible.

We were on the highway now, climbing Cemetery Hill. The car did it smoothly without Mikey having to shift gears. Uncle Josh chuckled and patted the dashboard. "Good old car. Listen to that engine. It's not even trying hard."

Aunt Sophia cleared her throat and turned a page in her Bible.

We moved along a three-mile stretch of straight road to the next town. My aunt's eyes flashed to the speedometer. Her pale hands gripped the gold-leafed book.

The speed of the Packard lured me forward to breathe into my cousin's shoulder. Another car appeared up ahead, and we were closing in on it. Mikey hung back a little. My aunt let out a breath.

My uncle said, "What're you sitting here for? Get around that thing."

Mikey pulled out into the other lane. My aunt turned another page. I wondered about the yellow line stretching up the next hill. The other driver did not want to be passed. We were still behind him. "Keep going," my uncle said. We were gaining on the car. The driver wore a big straw hat. He didn't give an inch. We were beside the car then, on that yellow line. A third car appeared at the top of the hill, coming down at us.

Aunt Sophia muttered, "Give us this day...."

We were not around the straw hat yet, and the third car kept coming. I could tell now it was a Ford. Uncle Josh said, "Give it some gas. Floor it!"

Aunt Sophie sucked in air. "Forgive us our debts as we forgive our debtors."

Mikey's hands were white on the wheel. The Packard surged forward. The driver in the Ford was coming at us, his eyes wide.

"Get around that guy," Uncle Josh yelled.

The approaching Ford braked and started to skid.

Aunt Sophie threw up her hands, knocking her Bible to the floor. "Oh Lord, oh Lord. Save us, save us."

Tires squealed as Mikey whipped the Packard over to the right lane. The Ford skittered by on the left. The driver stared straight ahead, his eyes like two fried eggs on a white plate.

Aunt Sophie picked up her Bible and sank back. Her head dropped against the seat.

Uncle Josh said, "Yessir, boy, never let 'em buffalo you."

Everyone was quiet after that. A little farther along Mikey turned off the highway onto a gravel road leading to a small white church surrounded by big oak trees.

When we emerged from the car, Uncle Joshua and Mikey smoothed their jackets and tightened their ties. Aunt Sophia straightened her skirt and clasped her Bible against her chest. Head high, combs glittering, she marched to the church. My short dress skimming my bare knees, I followed.

Chapter Eight

TRAIN TRIP TO AUNT BELLE'S

As long as I could remember, I liked the sound of train whistles. Maybe it started back in those barely-remembered years in the bungalow. Like something coming out of a dream, the whistle nudged me out of sleep, rolled me into a different position. With the lulling rhythm of the wheels, I drifted with the whistle into another dream.

There were times too—when I visited my grandmother—that I sneaked down to the tracks, standing close enough to feel the whoosh of air as the train whizzed past, watching people in dining cars streak along to a different world. That pounding wonder of going someplace new always had a greater pull on me than her warnings of "Stay back, or the wheels will suck you right in."

And now I was actually going to ride on a train. Here we were in the grimy station at Littleton waiting for it to arrive. No one else seemed as excited as I was. Nancy pretended to be, but I knew the thunder of the engines scared her. My mother didn't act very excited either, although the trip had been her idea.

She had surprised everyone by announcing at the breakfast table a few days before that she was going to visit Aunt Belle, and that she would take us kids with her—except Frankie. My father's eyes had jerked up from his fried eggs to stare at her. Then he raked his chair away from the table, got up, and was out the door.

Things were still out of sorts after the accident and the funeral. No one talked about Bruce anymore. His name became a word you weren't supposed to say. It was like watching a toy balloon getting bigger and bigger and waiting for it to pop. It was most likely to pop when my mother was talking to Frankie. I guessed my folks knew

about Frankie's fight. Now, every time he left the house, my mother
was on him about where he was going.

"I don't want you working on those machines," she said.

"I can drive the tractor as good as anyone," he said.

"You can pick up bundles or help your grandpa. Better yet, you can
help me around here."

She found jobs for him. "The fence in the chicken yard needs
fixing."

"I need some corn shelled."

"You can help me weed the garden."

"Ruth Ann can do that," Frankie complained.

"Let up on him, will you?" my father finally said.

My mother rounded on him. "You going to put him on top of one
of those loads?"

Frankie sulked around the house and barn lot, punching me or
pulling my hair whenever I got within two feet of him. My father went
off to the fields, staying late into the evening. His tractor or truck
pulled into the barn lot as Nancy and I settled into bed.

One night, after he had gone to choir practice, I was awakened by
my mother's voice. "Well, it's late enough. I suppose you and that
Bernice Elkins were practicing a duet or something."

"She brought in a cake, and some of us stayed and talked."

"A real party, then?"

"At least we could laugh a little."

"Sorry, I don't feel too much in a laughing mood."

Now we waited on the church-like benches in the railroad station.
My father sat with his head down, like he was studying the black
outlines of the tile. Nancy and Larry slid back and forth on the scruffy
seats. Mother kept watch on our stuff—a suitcase fastened with one of
Father's old belts plus a couple of paper-wrapped packages tied with
string.

Nancy climbed on his lap. "You going with us, Daddy?"

"This trip was your mom's idea," he said. "Besides, I got work to
do."

"But Daddy, you'll be lonely."

"Aunt Belle's got a big house, doesn't she?" I asked.

"To hear her tell it, she does."

My mother turned again to the clock over the station manager's
window.

"It'll be here soon enough," my father said. The blue vein that stood out on his temple moved like a squiggly worm.

At last the train whistle sounded, and there was the bustle to get everything together and out on the platform. My mother handed one of the packages to me. "Don't lose it now." She hitched Larry high on one hip, grabbed Nancy's hand, and turned to my father. "Look after Frankie."

"I'm not going to let anything happen to Frankie." He followed with the suitcase.

I rushed out to the platform where a ringing sound ran along the tracks, building like a roll of drums. The platform vibrated under my feet as the engine chugged to us, its noise shutting down our voices. Giant wheels ground out sparks and cinders, and as the engine belched out smoke mixed with steam, I tasted it on my tongue.

I was the first one up the train steps, only to wait on the iron grating, wondering which car we would go into. My mother was behind me. "Take Nancy's hand, please." She turned to grab the suitcase.

My father's question to her stuck in my mind: "You will be back, won't you?"

"I'll write you," she said. Then she pushed open the door and led us through.

I squeezed forward to find a seat next to the platform. On the other side of the window, my father stood waiting, watching. By the time my mother had settled the suitcase and packages and reversed the back of another seat so we could ride facing each other, he was no longer there.

The train creaked and lurched as couplings jolted together. The wail of the whistle rose high over other sounds of the train. Steam and smoke rolled between me and the town. Telephone poles ran faster and faster, stretching out arms to me, and the train sped into open country.

~ ~ ~

Aunt Belle and Uncle Lars met us at the station. In her floaty, gauzy dress, Aunt Belle seemed out of place among hot travelers pulling at their sweaty clothes as they collected scruffy suitcases from the baggage car. She gave my mother a quick hug and patted Larry on the back as he pushed a head of damp swirling hair against my mother's neck. Aunt Belle did not offer to take him. She was not one of those women who cooed over babies.

"We'll talk," said Aunt Belle, giving Larry another pat. She draped her arms lightly around Nancy's shoulders and mine.

Aunt Belle was tall and slender. With the afternoon sun lighting the curls of her brown hair, she looked like a girl next to my mother. "How was the train ride?" she asked.

My hand went to my own hair and pushed back a long strand that had fallen across my bangs. "It was great. The conductor—he was nice—he took me and Nancy out on the caboose platform—that's at the very end of the train—so we could really see."

"It went fast," Nancy interrupted. "Larry was scared. He kept crying and crying."

"The rails were like shiny ribbons spinning out beneath us," I said. "When we went past a farm or through towns, people would wave— like they wanted to be on the train too."

I stopped talking when Uncle Lars looked at me, cross-like. He wore a white shirt with rolled-up sleeves and dark pants, like those my father wore to church. Except for his dark eyes behind wire-rimmed glasses, everything about him was pale, from his blond hair lifting off his pink scalp to his winter-white fingers reaching for my mother's suitcase. I remembered my father calling him a city fella who didn't know about getting dirt under his fingernails.

Uncle Lars led us to a gleaming, green car with a silver-spoked wheel set in the front fender.

"Where's the top, Uncle Lars?" Nancy asked. "Did your car get broken?"

He glanced at her and did not smile.

I punched Nancy. "It's a convertible, silly." I had seen pictures of them in one of Frankie's car magazines.

After putting our suitcase and paper-wrapped bags in the bumped-out boot, Uncle Lars opened one of the doors and lifted Nancy onto the running board.

"Grandpa has a buggy like this," Nancy said. I scrambled across the leather seat and punched her again.

My mother slid in beside us, holding Larry on her lap. Aunt Belle pushed a long, fair arm along the back of the front seat and turned to smile at us. "We just bought the car."

"The only one like it in town." Uncle Lars gave a brief nod to some men who stood gawking at us.

"It's very nice." My mother settled Larry on the seat. He let out a sharp cry.

"The seat burns his legs," Nancy said. "Mine too."

My mother took short-panted Larry back onto her lap.

I hissed at Nancy, "Stop being such a sissy."

The car started to glide away from the station. My mother leaned back against the cushions, and for the first time since we had left home, a real smile showed on her face.

I sat up as tall as I could. This was me, not Frankie, riding in this grand car.

We drove past the band shell in the city park where boys playing marbles on the dusty ground stood to stare at us, and old men on benches woke from their naps. It was like we were in a parade.

We entered a side street where the roofs of houses disappeared in the trees, and soon Uncle Lars pulled into the driveway of a large white house. A series of black screen porches belted the house, like a square old lady wearing a dirty apron.

"It's an old house, you see," Aunt Belle said.

"Historic, actually. One of the first great houses in town," said Uncle Lars. "Those porches are going to come off."

A tall square tower rose above one of the porches. Glints of sunlight flashed against stained glass windows under its pointed roof. "It's watching us," I said.

Uncle Lars laughed. "And it's getting a damned good view from up there. But that's private territory. Not ready for company."

My mother nodded to a small "Room for Rent" sign posted near the door. "Not all of your rooms are rented?"

"All but one," said Aunt Belle. "We had to ask the man to leave. Always hounding the others about the bathroom and leaving it in a mess."

Uncle Lars ushered us through a side entrance into an enclosed hallway. It seemed dark after being outside in the sun. After a minute or two, I made out the dark polished wood of a stair rail reaching up on one side of the hallway and dusky, figured wallpaper on the other.

My mother's eyes followed the carpeted steps rising upward. "Is this the entrance your roomers use?"

"Oh, no." Aunt Belle laughed. "There's a back entrance and stairway. They use that. My piano students and Lars' patients use this door." She nodded to another door marked *DOCTOR'S OFFICE* opposite the stairs. "A lot of traffic in this house."

"That's why we have to stay put on the main floor." Uncle Lars looked directly at Nancy and me.

My mother asked questions about the roomers. I wondered what use it was to have these rooms if you couldn't go into them. At the top of the stairs, colored beams of light moved through a round, stained-glass window. The tower's up there somewhere, I thought.

Uncle Lars unlocked the door at the end of the hall, and we entered a large square room. A long, lace-covered table stood in front of a marble fireplace. Tall, straight, no-squirming-allowed chairs guarded the table. There were plates everywhere. Not on the table, but on the walls. Plates in a sort of faded red showed little towers and tiny people on arched bridges. On others, gold rims encircled pretty flowers or birds. I couldn't imagine eating off those plates. A large china cabinet took up one wall, but there were no dishes in it, only fancy figurines.

The living room, as big as our house back home, stretched out from the dining room. I caught only a blurred impression of lots of furniture and two pianos as Aunt Belle led us through the kitchen to a room behind it. We stepped down into a smallish room with a bank of windows and rather roughly painted floor and walls.

"We call it the dog house," Uncle Lars laughed. "It's a porch we're doing over."

A double bed and small chest took up most of the room. A cot was wedged against one wall.

"Sorry, it won't work out to put you upstairs," Aunt Belle said. "I hope you'll be comfortable here."

Chapter Nine

ALL THESE ROOMS

I liked the room. With its wood floor and walls and trees brushing the windows, it was like sleeping outside or maybe in a cabin. Curtains billowed gently at the open windows as grayish-green dawn crept in. But I didn't like staying in bed while others slept. Besides, I was tired of Nancy's knees poking me in the back. On the other side of Nancy, my mother was still asleep, so she couldn't tell me to stay in bed. I pushed the sheet aside and snuck into the kitchen. In spite of the dim light, everything shone white in the room—the sink, a real refrigerator that didn't use ice, and a stove that you didn't have to carry cobs for. White fluffy curtains with red polka dots hung at the window. Patterned wallpaper and colorful plates surrounded the white cupboards. It was like a picture in a magazine.

As pretty as it was, the kitchen offered me nothing to do. I walked past the stiff dining room chairs to the living room. A tall clock, taller even than Uncle Lars, stood in one corner. The gold disk of the pendulum went back and forth. From the face of the clock, a smiling moon looked back at me. I jumped as the clock started to strike. That was bound to wake everyone up. Another clock struck and another. It was funny how they weren't together.

Large pictures and more plates leaned in from the walls, and lamps stood like trees next to covered tables and cushiony chairs. It was very grand, but the dusty smell reminded me a little of the Benz parlor—a room not to be used. Vases and figurines crowded together on tables. Others paraded across the grand piano and the smaller one. I edged in close to one pretty thing then another, keeping my hands clenched behind me. A hundred times, my mother had warned, "Don't touch anything, or we're likely to be sent home on the next train."

I was bending forward to study a small dancer whose skirts were a swirl of rose and gold, when a voice spoke from behind me. "Ruth Ann."

Almost losing my balance, I spun around. My aunt stood in the doorway. "I didn't touch anything, really."

Aunt Belle stepped forward, her long dressing gown making soft, swishing sounds. She picked up the figurine and held it firmly to me.

"It's beautiful, isn't it? Feel how smooth it is, how delicate each rosette on her gown, the curls of her hair. Gently now. I'm glad you didn't bother it. It's Dresden, very special. If it were broken, I probably could never find another one like it."

I pulled my hands back. The room seemed stuffed with dolls like this one, but if Aunt Belle said so, I supposed it was different. Carefully, Aunt Belle placed the figure back on the table. "Couldn't you sleep?"

"Nancy kept kicking me all night long. She always does that."

"I'm sorry. I know it was a bit crowded for you. Your uncle has gone out for the paper and some milk, so why don't you help me get breakfast? But first, go into the bathroom and wash your hands and face."

I entered the bathroom off the kitchen and closed the door behind me. Compared to our outhouse, this bathroom was a whole different place. Pale green tile gave it a cool feeling, and it smelled so clean with its perfumed soap and freshly laundered towels. Waves of sunlight streamed through a glass brick window, making everything watery, especially the opposite wall where swans swam through bulrushes. It made me think of Sunday School story books about baby Moses.

On racks, white washcloths and towels with tiny embroidered roses hung just so over large green towels. And there was real toilet paper and a real bathtub on claw feet. I stood on tiptoe to see myself in the mirror above the sink. As usual, my hair bushed out like a mop. I used my fingers to smooth it down. In such a house, I had to look my best.

Hot water nearly burned my hands when I turned on one of the faucets. At home on the farm, hot water came only from the teakettle on the range. I tried the other faucet and let cool water stream over my hands. A bar of scented soap felt smooth, not like the grainy Lava soap we used at home. Certain that those embroidered washcloths were only for show, I splashed cold water on my face. Trying not to disturb the straight folds of the towels, I was lifting the corner of one when someone pounded on the door.

"Ruth Ann, I gotta go, quick!"

"Hold your horses." I opened the door to find Nancy prancing foot to foot.

"You took all day." Hitching up her nightgown, she rushed past me.

"Don't make a mess," I called back and closed the door.

At breakfast, everything went wrong. My mother would not let us go to the table in our nightclothes. Saying we had to be presentable, she opened her small suitcase and groaned at the sight of the clothes she had washed, starched, and ironed, now wrinkled. She tried to smooth out dresses for Nancy and me before tugging a clean shirt over Larry's head. In the kitchen, Aunt Belle's heels clicked back and forth.

We presented ourselves just as Uncle Lars growled, "Those eggs are going to be as hard as rocks." After a search for two Sears Roebuck catalogs for Larry to sit on, we were finally seated around the kitchen table.

My mother took a deep breath and let her gaze sweep the table. "Isn't this pretty, girls? Just the way a table should look. You shouldn't have gone to so much trouble, Belle."

Uncle Lars rattled off a grace before I had time to close my eyes to the stack of plates in front of me. On the top plate was half of a very large lemon centered with a red cherry.

"The children haven't had grapefruit before," my mother said, grabbing Larry's hand as he reached for the cherry on her fruit.

"I thought it would be a treat," said Aunt Belle. "I cut them into sections. Use your spoons. Like this." She looked at me then Nancy who had already eaten her cherry and was spooning the grapefruit into her mouth. She scrunched up her face. "I don't like it."

"Let's try some sugar on it." My mother sprinkled some on Nancy's fruit.

"No, I don't like it." Nancy shoved the plate back. It teetered on top of the other dishes. Aunt Belle jumped up and moved the dish to the safety of the counter.

Uncle Lars made quick work of his grapefruit with sure jabs of his spoon. Trying to follow his example, I took a firm grip on the fruit before me and got a good squirt in the eye. After my first taste, I helped myself to sugar, scattering much of it over my plate and silverware. Determined to show my aunt and uncle I was grown up enough to handle this special treat, I dug at it more firmly. The fruit flipped off my plate, left sugary streaks across my clean dress, and plopped face down on the floor. My mother was on her feet, scooping up the grapefruit, then on her hands and knees with a towel mopping up.

"Ruth Ann made a mess," Nancy said.

"Shut up," I hissed.

"Let's try some oatmeal." Aunt Belle rose to ladle great bowls of it. I stared at my empty plate while the grown-ups filled the silence with talk about the weather, the roomers upstairs. Aunt Belle asked my mother about how she could think of taking on anything more—with us kids and all. My mother said she had to do something.

Uncle Lars asked, "What is Dan going to do about this?"

I looked up as she shrugged. "I guess I'll find out."

What my mother would find out I never learned just then for Larry slipped off his catalogs sending his milk flying. She was down on her hands and knees again after an aside to me, "Watch Larry."

~ ~ ~

For the next couple of days, I spent a lot of my time watching Larry. The house was big and grand, but there was no place for Larry to crawl or play with Nancy and me. There was plenty for Larry to reach for and grab—all those shiny things on tasseled table covers. Aunt Belle gasped in alarm as small tables rocked. Nancy and I tried playing hide and seek in the forest of furniture, but Aunt Belle's stern looks took the fun out of that.

Only the back yard with its green lawn and apple tree to climb offered an escape from fine objects turned into no-nos. Our trips back into the house for the bathroom or drinks of water interrupted my mother and Aunt Belle talking about money or the roomers upstairs. I didn't understand this talk about roomers, since I never saw them.

One afternoon while Larry and Nancy napped in the doghouse, I got bored being outside by myself. With no audience, my hanging upside down from the apple tree was no fun. Returning to the house, I heard music coming from the living room. My mother sat at the grand piano. Her large hands that often held a garden hoe or buckets of water now moved with the free flight of birds. The lift of my mother's head, the smile on her face, made me think of the picture at my grandmother's house—the teenage girl, dark hair curling over her shoulders, white dress flowing over the piano bench. My mother was in a happy place I had no part of.

I tiptoed to the far side of the room and eased myself into a barrel-shaped chair that faced away from the piano. Listening to the notes that rippled from her fingers, I too was in a different place—sitting beside our pasture creek, the water rising and falling, rushing over rocks and gliding away.

Aunt Belle entered the room quietly, but my mother seemed to know she was there. Her fingers became just fingers again, unable to make music.

"Very nice," Aunt Belle said. "I haven't heard you play for a long time."

"Your students must be thrilled to play this piano." My mother's hands caressed the keys.

"Only the very best play this one. The others play the spinet."

"Oh," she said and closed the piano lid. The young girl in my picture disappeared.

"I didn't mean...," started Aunt Belle.

"I'm way out of practice," my mother said, but her fingers lingered on the polished wood.

"You do still have your piano, don't you?"

"Catches dust mostly. It hasn't been tuned in ages."

"Mother said you gave up the pianist job at your church."

"I didn't feel much like going back after Larry was born, and there was all that talk. I'm sure Mother filled you in on that."

"You mean about the death of that boy? But it was an accident, wasn't it?"

"Talk had already started on another front." My mother paused, and the next words came from deep in her throat. "I tried to tell myself it was Dan being Dan—a little sweet-talking, a little flirting during choir." She paused again. "One or two kind souls decided it was their duty to enlighten me."

"Who is this woman?"

"Bernice Elkins. You know, she's from that no 'count Newman family. Well, her husband died two or three years ago, and she's been cozying up to every man ever since."

Bernice Elkins. The name rang in my head. Some women at church tittered behind their hands about her. About that woman and my father? Well, they were just liars. That's all. He was kidding around, like he always did.

I tiptoed away from my chair. I wanted to get out of that room where things should not be touched and words should not be heard.

But once in the hallway, I didn't know which way to go. Escaping to the back yard meant going through the doghouse where Nancy and Larry were napping. The front door was out since it opened off the living room. The door down the hall and next to the stairs led to the street, always busy and noisy with cars. At the top of the stairs colored beams of light from the stained-glass window winked at me.

When I reached the top, I found the door to the attic open. I remembered that Uncle Lars had been working up there. In spite of his pale, soft-looking hands, when he was not with patients in his office, he was busy building or fixing something in the old house. His carpentry erected more reasons for keeping us children out of his way. "Kids don't know enough to watch for nails or splinters," he said. "Besides they break things faster than you can fix them."

Inside the door, a walled stairway led upward. I remembered that Uncle Lars had left the house to purchase something at the hardware store. This was my chance to really explore the tower. I climbed the rough, unpainted steps. The stairwell opened onto a space that took my breath away. It was as big and open as the hayloft in our barn, maybe as big as a field. Uncle Lars' newly laid floor stretched from wall to wall. Around the walls were several windows and brick chimneys from the fireplaces below reaching up to a partial ceiling. Wind sighed through the upper reaches of the beams and rafters. My footsteps echoed across the wood floor and around piles of old boards and stacks of cast-off window frames and screens. I wondered if my mother or Aunt Belle heard me downstairs.

Along the far end of the wall, light beckoned above another set of steps. They seemed to lead right through the roof. That must be the tower. The steps were unevenly spaced and surprisingly steep. Worst yet, there was no handrail to hang onto. A few more steps, and I was above the roofline, inside the tower. At the base, beneath the group of windows, ran a narrow platform, something like the catwalk in the cupola of our barn, a place where only Frankie dared to go. A show-off as usual, he would scare us by swinging his arms as if about to fall.

If Frankie could do it, I could do it too. Grabbing a jutting section of the window framework, I stepped onto the platform and inched forward to look out the windows.

The glass was clouded with dirt, and I swiped my hand across the pane. Even then, I could barely see the building across the street. The windows curved outward, and no matter how hard I rubbed at the glass, the house across the street was still blurred, bulging and shrinking as if it were about to fall.

The tower sure wasn't much. I might as well go back down since I couldn't see anything. If Uncle Lars caught me up here, I'd be in big trouble. From the narrow platform the attic floor looked a long way down. How did I climb so high? Forcing myself to pull away from the tower wall and let go of the window frame, I stood atop those steps. There was nothing to hang onto. I edged one foot down to the first step, then another and another. The next step was much bigger than I expected. I flailed for balance, for something to grab hold of. I was falling to Uncle Lars' new floor. He would be very angry.

Chapter Ten

THINGS BROKEN

I guarded my arm, cradling the cast in the tea-towel sling my mother had made for it. Standing at the edge of the chicken yard and watching her swing the axe again and again, I almost felt the jolt of the blade against the tree stump. Since our hurried return from Aunt Belle's, my mother was out there every morning, swinging that axe. I was sure she had to kill, dress, and sell so many chickens because of the doctor's bill for setting my arm.

The last couple of days at Aunt Belle's blurred together like the scene outside the tower windows. I remembered turning away from those windows and having nothing to hold onto. It was almost like falling into water that sucked me under and tossed me to something that hurt awful. Somewhere between that nothingness and pain, the flash of Uncle Lars' arms reached for me. There was nothing again. Then I felt myself eased onto a sofa. Not Aunt Belle's sofa, I thought. I'll get it dirty.

My mother, Aunt Belle, and Nancy hovered nearby. From the look on their faces, I must have been nearly killed. Maybe like Bruce.

Uncle Lars told them how he had found me, my body clumped over my twisted arm. It seemed like some wild animal was yanking on my arm. Everything about it hurt. Uncle Lars touched the new bend in it, and I screamed.

"It's broken," he said. "I'll fix a sling for it, and we'll drive her to the doctor."

"But you're a doctor," I said. My tears overflowed Aunt Belle's embroidered cushions.

My next sensations were of being held in my mother's arms, how even the jostling of the car hurt. Everything blurred again to a closed-in place with sickly green walls, something that smelled like medicine, and to the hard, cold table beneath me.

Eyes surrounded by black hair peered down at me. Like a huge dog, a red mouth opened in a black, curly beard. "This is going to hurt a little," the mouth said. His quick pull on my arm knifed through me. There was a pop. I screamed and screamed some more.

Back at the house, Nancy and Larry could not keep their hands off my cast. After saying, "She'll be all right," Uncle Lars stayed his distance, but Aunt Belle and my mother urged me to rest. Aunt Belle made cookies for me. They didn't fuss over me all the time. Sometimes my mother and Aunt Belle forgot about me and huddled over the table talking about things like room rents, costs for heat, and electricity. And for some reason, Aunt Belle kept telling my mother to be careful, to think everything out.

A couple of days later my mother was on the phone making arrangements to take the next train home. As we left the following day, I noted the doctor sign outside the door. Under Uncle Lars' name was the word *Chiropractor*. I decided to ask her about it later.

But I didn't ask about it. Questions didn't seem in order. All the way home, my mother sat quietly next to the train window, her gaze fixed on open fields, hemmed in by trees and fences.

In my own corner, I protected my arm, afraid of bumps from Nancy or Larry. It would be good to get home.

My father and Frankie were waiting on the platform as our train rolled in. My father put his arms around my mother. She stood stiffly, holding Larry between them. There was a question in my father's eyes as he stepped back and turned to hug Nancy and me. He gave me an extra squeeze and patted my cast. "A pretty strong arm you've got there. You can fend off Frankie with that."

Frankie asked a single question: "Does it hurt?" After that, he called me clumsy and accused me of wanting to get out of chores.

I wanted to show my mother that wasn't true. Watching a headless chicken in its last twirl across the ground, I steeled myself to clutch its twitching legs with my one good hand and place the carcass in the washtub. I decided I hated chickens. Live ones, anyway. I wasn't ready to give up on my battle with Frankie for the wishbone at our Sunday dinners.

It was hard to help my mother much with one arm. And no matter what I did, she acted worried. No matter how hard I tried not to upset

her and my father by doing my chores on time and putting up with
Larry and Nancy always pestering me, I could not stop my parents'
arguments. Often, they woke me after Nancy and I had gone to bed.
One quarrel had started just as I helped Nancy clear the supper table.
Frankie had gone out to the well to bring in some water, and Larry was
pushing a wooden truck around on the floor. I nearly stumbled over
Larry when I heard my mother's question.

"What if Shaffer sells this farm?"

"I ain't heard nothing about that." My father didn't sound too
concerned.

"We could be the last to hear. Like at that last place."

He didn't say anything, just broke up pieces of bread to stir into his
glass of milk.

"Maybe we should look around for another place," she said.

He spooned sugar into his milk. "This is good land. Crops are extra
good this year."

"Land is not everything. We need a decent house. It'd be nice to
have electric lights and running water."

"No farms 'round here like that. I heard no talk about Shaffer
selling." He scraped sugar from the bottom of his glass. "Might as well
leave 'nough be."

"It'd be good to get Frankie away from this accident talk. I can't
help thinking about that fight at the Jamboree. There may have been
others for all we know."

"Frankie's not going to be in any more fights," he said.

Later, I rolled over in bed, nudged awake by voices in the living
room. I could not make out the words, but my mother sounded a little
like Nancy begging.

His voice bounded back. "What am I supposed to do in town?"

My mother's words were clear now. "You could work in a garage.
You're good with machines."

"You mean in some shed-like shop. With a boss looking over my
shoulder?"

Her answer was quick and sharp. "Well, with all of us crowding
around the stove trying to keep warm, winter in this house is not much
better than being in a shed."

"I ain't moving to no town."

"You sure it's farm life holding you here? Not some other
attraction?"

"Who feeds you that stuff? It's plain and simple. I ain't moving to no town."

It was weeks later before I heard those words again. Summer droned on. Flies clung to the screen door and the oilcloth on the table. There were nights when Nancy and I ran through drying grass to capture lightning bugs and put them in fruit jars—if my mother would let us punch holes in her carefully counted out lids. The next morning we woke up scratching at chigger bites raising ugly red welts around our waists and ankles.

Most days my mother was busy with canning or killing and dressing chickens, and I got the job of watching Larry. There were also days when she would take Larry and go off with Uncle Stu, leaving Frankie to watch me and Nancy. Frankie complained about being stuck with two little kids when he wanted to go out with my father. She said my father would have to get along without Frankie because she needed him to stay with us.

Frankie wasn't much of a watcher. He only sat around picking on the guitar Aunt Belle had given him the Christmas before. He'd done that a lot since the threshing accident. No one ever said "the day Bruce was killed"—it was just *the accident.* Frankie didn't pay any attention to me teasing Nancy. So that was no fun.

And I kept getting stuck with Frankie's chores. As usual, he was off somewhere. I didn't really mind going to the barn for cobs. I was glad to get away from the hot kitchen and my mother too, who was cranky most of the time. Maybe it was all the canning she did—like she was storing up for something.

But on that day, I didn't like what I found in the barn. As I stepped inside to the hay-covered floor, I heard Frankie's voice. "She says she's leaving."

Who was he talking about? And why was Frankie here in the barn, not out in the field?

I forgot about the cobs and hung back, behind the hay chute. It was my father who answered: "She's just talking."

Frankie said, "She goes into Centerville with Uncle Stu every chance she gets."

My father stood by a rough bench where we set milk buckets and stuff. "Your ma always did have a thing for going to town."

"But she's looking at houses to rent."

"Who told you that?"

"I hear things."

I peeked around the hay chute past the feeding troughs. Frankie stayed next to the ladder leading to the loft. He didn't look like the same boy who would snake his way up that ladder, grab the barn rope hanging from the upper curve of the haymow, and swing as high as he could above mounds of hay.

"What if she really means to go?" he asked.

My father picked his hat up off the bench and used it to brush at something on his pant leg.

Frankie's voice came again. "Will you come with us?"

"Us? She been after you?"

"Mom expects me to go. What am I supposed to do?"

"She had no business bringing you into it." My father sank down on the bench. His hands moved across his lap like he didn't know what to do with them. "I reckon you'll do what you do."

"Will you come with us?"

"I ain't moving to no town." He sat there, not saying anything. Then he stood up. "We got to get back to the field."

Frankie took hold of the ladder, like he needed something to hang onto. "Dad, is Mom leaving because of that woman?"

My father whirled to face him. "What're you talking about?"

"I hear the guys… what they say."

"No use you listening to such talk."

"I seen things too—like you're great pals with that choir woman."

"Don't you be making things up, boy."

"Then you'll move with us?"

"I'm going back to the field. That's what I'm going to do. Are you coming or not?" My father clapped his hat on his head and marched out the back door of the barn.

I heard the hoopie rev up. I supposed Frankie followed him, but I hurried to the front of the corncrib where cobs were piled. I filled my basket as quick as I could. I didn't want my mother to leave me. She did go to Centerville a lot with Uncle Stu, but she always came back. And my father said we weren't moving. Frankie didn't know what he was talking about.

PART TWO
TOWN

Chapter Eleven

A HOUSE NEAR THE SQUARE

"Your mother's moving you into Centerville." I hadn't really believed my grandmother's words when I heard them at breakfast, but it was almost noon and my grandfather's car was entering what he called our county-seat town.

The twenty-mile trip was one that he made only in good weather. My grandmother's wanting to wander through fancy stores to buy something way too expensive was not worth his getting stuck on the mud road between his farm and the highway.

As the Nash rolled along one side of the elm-shaded courthouse square, I remembered someone calling it "the biggest town square in the world." The person had spoken with such authority and pride that I believed him. Nancy and I twisted our heads to see the dime stores across from the courthouse. Earlier in the summer we had spent many a Saturday browsing in those stores while waiting for my mother to finish her shopping. I supposed she had looked through the town's dress shops and the dry goods store, but the only packages she carried at the end of each day were from the grocery store.

A recent Saturday in town was pretty much like the others. With our father waiting for us outside or talking to the men he knew in town, Nancy and I had been free to wander through the dime stores where counters lay before us like giant dress-up boxes. When the clerks were busy with other customers, we tried on bracelets and rings, preened before small mirrors, used imaginary dabs from blue bottles of *Evening in Paris* perfume, spread our fingers, and pursed our lips for the pretend gloss of nail polish and lipstick in pale pinks or fuchsia. We didn't dare do this if my grandmother was even aisles away. Dead set against cosmetics, she declared that no one in her family was going to paint herself like some savage. However, I had never heard her say a word against Aunt Belle's use of rouge or nail polish.

I imagined myself being one of the red-lipped teenage girls who straddled stools at the soda fountain. Bracelets dangled and clicked from their wrists as they dipped straws in frosty glasses. Giggling and chattering, they sneaked glances at the mirror checking reflections of themselves.

If I could live in town, wear clothes like theirs, I'd be like them, sure of myself, and no one would look down on me. One of the leggy teenagers twirled her stool around and with a glare over her drink directed loud, slurping noises at me. I backed off and grabbed Nancy away from the candy counter. "Why you standing here like a loony?" Nancy squealed that I was the loony, but she followed me to the back of the store.

"Look at all the Mickey birds." Nancy pointed to black and yellow birds bumping against their cages.

"They're canaries, silly. Grandma's bird is just named Mickey."

Nancy turned to the aquariums of goldfish. Wide-eyed, she watched a salesgirl scoop up a fish with a ladle and deposit it in a small paper bucket for a waiting customer. I wandered into an area where other customers thumbed through sheet music and "song hits" magazines. Behind the racks of music, a girl sat at a piano, picking at chipped red polish on her fingernails. A customer handed her sheets of music and said, "I need to hear this." The girl swiped her blond hair from her eyes and played the tune. Her whole body kept time, and I found myself swaying along with her.

When Nancy and I returned to the front of the store, the clock in the courthouse tower told me it was time for us to meet my mother. I remembered to hold Nancy's hand as we crossed the broad street and dropped it once we were inside the large stone building. Our footsteps thumped hollow along the cool, marble hall as we walked to our meeting place, the women's waiting room next to the restroom. The sound and smell of johns flushing didn't seem to bother the women and children who waited there, relaxing on oak chairs and benches. Nancy plopped down in a rocking chair, and I squeezed in beside her. We rocked gently, our eyes taking in the other people in the room.

A woman, probably as old as my grandmother, sat near the lamp table knitting. Her needles clicked together faster as she studied us. "Where's your mother? Are you two girls alone?"

Unsure what to say, I said nothing. Two other women by the window barely glanced at us. One was saying, "She calls herself my friend, but you can't believe what she had the nerve to tell me...." The second one bent forward to hear, ignoring the tussle between two children on a nearby bench until one landed on the floor screaming.

With scarcely a pause in her story—"well, you can guess what I told her..."—the first woman scooped up the child who immediately hushed and squirmed away to climb back onto the bench. This gave the knitter something else to click her needles over, but her eyes swung back to Nancy and me when our mother came in.

She looked "played out" as she often said following an afternoon of gardening. The dress she had recently sewn for herself was wrinkled and pulled off her shoulder where Larry lay sleeping.

"Did you get us something?" Nancy asked.

"No, honey. I bought groceries. We'll pick them up later." She sighed. "Let me sit there, will you?" She eased us out of the rocker. "I need to feed Larry before we leave."

Soon we were packed again inside the cab of my father's truck, on our way out of town. Her eyes turned to the big houses on Grand Avenue. "I don't see why we can't live in town," she said to my father. "You could find some kind of work here."

His voice came back with the same I had heard before. "I ain't going to live in no town."

~ ~ ~

But evidently we were going to live in town. A couple of blocks from the square, my grandfather pulled his Nash into an alley next to Uncle Stu's truck parked behind a two-story yellow house. Uncle Stu and Frankie were there, wrestling a bedstead out of the truck.

Tall and hard-muscled like his father, Uncle Stu also had his slow step. My father had once said, "Your grandpa might step slow, but he's always taking that step. He gets to where he wants to go. Stu's steps just go in a circle." I remembered times we had driven past Uncle Stu's farm and seen the barn he had started to build years before, and each time my father would shake his head. "It ain't fallen down yet, but it's leaning."

My grandfather emerged slowly from his car and stood with one hand braced against the hood, looking at the house. I could tell he didn't like it much.

"Can't you give Stuart a hand, Dad?" My grandmother's voice broke across his study of the cindered path that led to the back stoop.

"This is it, huh?" His eyes lifted to the second-floor windows and the paint peeling from their frames. "It's going to take a train load of coal to heat this place." He shook his head and went to drag boxes out of the truck.

I followed Nancy and my grandmother across the narrow stoop and into the kitchen. Its chill and dim light made me think of her cellar. My mother was in the kitchen surrounded by boxes. Holding Larry in one arm, she barely paused as she swung open doors of dark cupboards and pushed jars of green beans, tomatoes, and corn onto shelves.

"There's so much space," my mother said. "I don't have to put my canned goods down in a cellar."

"They would keep better in a cellar," my grandmother muttered. She grabbed a dishcloth and washed out the cupboards before my mother could fill them.

"Let me get this box unpacked and I'll show you around. There's electricity and water—a bathroom upstairs and another down here. Of course, I'll rent out the upstairs. Like Belle does." My mother talked fast, sounding breathless. I talked like that too, when I wanted something.

"And you have to furnish those upstairs rooms?" my grandfather asked.

"That's what the loan was for, Dad. But with the roomers, I'll have money coming in. Enough to pay you back in a few months."

Frankie carried in a box and set it down on top of others.

My grandfather wasn't finished with his worrying. "You said you had a furnace?"

"Yes, a real furnace in the basement. It's to heat the whole house."

"Do you know how it works?"

"It's a bit of a monster. I can't cope with that right now."

Frankie poked Nancy. "Did you hear that? There's a monster in the basement."

"Frankie, shame on you," my grandmother said. Nancy, her eyes round, edged closer to our mother.

"Make yourself useful, Frankie, and carry some of these boxes upstairs," my mother said. She turned to my grandfather. "We'll surely have a little time before cold weather sets in."

"It'll be here before you know it. Do you have any coal?"

Larry squirmed and fussed in her arms. She jostled him up and down. "I'm hoping Dan will bring me some."

My grandmother paused from scrubbing the sink. "He'll have to help you out some way."

"I doubt that Dan is in any mood to bring her coal now," my grandfather said.

Uncle Stu set down the box of pots and pans he'd brought in. "I'll pick up a load for you. Enough to tide you over until you can talk to Dan."

I wandered into the next room, away from the confusing talk about my father. If they wanted to talk to him, why didn't they just talk to him? Frankie yelled from the top of the stairs. "Mom, where do I put this stuff?"

"What is it?" she called back.

"I don't know—some of Ruth Ann's junk, I guess."

"You stay out of my things," I yelled and took off running.

With Frankie egging us on, Nancy and I discovered a lot of running space in the house—up the front stairs, across the landing, up more steps to the upper hall, then down the back stairs. Steep and dark, those steps slowed us down some. "Careful on those stairs," our mother called out.

There were hiding places too. Frankie found them and made a game of popping out of the oak-enclosed cupboard under the front stairs or the closets in the three upstairs bedrooms. Shrieking in delighted terror, Nancy ran from room to room slamming doors behind her.

My mother's voice came from the bottom of the stairs: "Frankie, Ruth Ann, settle down. I don't want to have to come up there."

She never yells at Nancy, I thought, tiring of the game. I went into the front bedroom, still empty of furniture, and stood looking out over the street littered with yellow maple leaves.

Nancy came to my side. "Do you see Daddy coming?"

I caught a glimpse of Frankie about to sneak into the room. Whatever trick he was planning, he changed his mind, turned without a word and went downstairs.

Chapter Twelve

PEOPLE BEHIND DOORS

On those first days when the sun spilled into the rooms through wide windows, slid down the wood rails of the staircase and splashed gold on the oak floor and woodwork, I knew the yellow house could be grand. My mother probably thought so too. Instead of working in the garden or the chicken yard, she was planning and making lists, hanging curtains in this big house, going to the sale barn or the second-hand store. She and Uncle Stu would return with her purchases about the time Nancy and I got home from school.

Helping Uncle Stu unload stuff, Frankie complained it was bad enough we had to live spitting distance from strangers, but now our mother was going to have them move in with us. Uncle Stu told him it must be some dumb idea she got from Aunt Belle.

I'd rush home from school to those rooms my mother fixed up for other people, but I found nothing new or shiny, only used metal beds and dressers and washbasins placed baldly against walls. As she added mismatched tables and chairs and kerosene burners, we kids were told to stay out—no more chasing each other through one door and out the other. I did not care much. The colorless cast-off furniture gave the rooms a lonesome feel. Days went by, and I came home to find that strangers had moved into the rooms and the doors were closed.

A Mr. Hamlin was the first to move in, his suitcases bulging and tied with binder twine. Frankie helped him carry in a smelly upholstered chair and boxes of books and newspapers. That smell hit me every time I came into the house after playing outside in crisp, autumn air. Some mornings Mr. Hamlin's steps sounded slow and heavy on the back stairs. He paused on the stoop, wound the brown wool scarf more tightly around his neck—although it wasn't even cold yet—and pulled a gray wide-brimmed hat over his eyes. In his long dark coat he became a gray stick of a man crunching his way to the square down the cindered path.

My mother said he usually came back mid-morning carrying a thick roll of newspapers. He left again in the afternoon with letters to mail. He always appeared dressed for town although he'd been a farmer. "He owned lots of land," she said. "He lost it in the Depression."

A Chicago newspaper was left on the front porch for him every evening. It was my job to take it upstairs to him. Approaching his room, I sometimes heard abrupt snorts of laughter and blurted talk. Someone was visiting him, someone he didn't like much. But when he opened the door to my knock, there was only his radio. I recognized the voice of a man my grandfather called Kaltenborn.

"Such nonsense," Mr. Hamlin barely paused to notice me, "telling how Roosevelt put all those people back to work. Him with his WPA. I see them around town, leaning on their shovels. Suppose this paper is saying more of the same." He turned back to the radio. "Thanks, girl." He closed the door.

As Mr. Hamlin became more accustomed to my bringing his paper, he would call out for me to come in. He had moved his one lamp next to his table, and I often found him there studying a newspaper as he wrote. Handing him still another paper, I saw he had written many pages.

One time when I came to his room, I could barely get the door open. It was blocked by a bunch of papers. Mr. Hamlin sat on the floor surrounded by them. His grasshopper legs folded under him, he attacked a newspaper with scissors.

"Washington's saying the Depression is over. Just flip through those scrapbooks." He waved his scissors to stacks of books on the floor and on the bed. "You'll see different. They're hiding the stories about us that lost everything on the back pages. They won't print my letters anymore."

He paused and actually looked at me. "Your ma said you folks lost your farm?"

I tried to remember. "Back when I was little. We've lived different places."

"The whole country's become a bunch of nomads. Or they're standing in line waiting for a handout. I'd die before I'd do that."

He picked up the paper I had brought him. "Everything's Europe and Hitler now. What is the age of that brother of yours?"

"You mean Frankie? He's fourteen."

"Maybe this mess in Europe will be cleared up before he gets old enough."

I didn't know what Europe or Hitler had to do with Frankie. I just wanted to get the door shut behind me, away from the smell of his cigarettes and his musty old chair.

A married couple had moved into the other front bedroom. My mother said she'd seen the husband early in the morning leaving with his sample case. He was some kind of a salesman, she thought.

His wife—she was young and pretty—did not emerge from their room until late morning. My mother would gripe about how she'd just get the bathroom cleaned up after the other roomers when the woman would take it over and leave it in a worse mess than before.

Frequently, as I helped my mother prepare supper, the lady would come down the front stairs dressed to go out. With that Betty Grable look, blond curls piled high above her forehead and falling in waves around her shoulders, she was like someone out of a movie. My mother's eyes traveled over the long slim skirt and high heels, her hand going to her own thick black hair, pushing it back from her face and brushing away the flour that smeared her print dress. When the weather turned cooler, the lady appeared in a fitted coat with a fox draped around her neck. My mother told Nancy and me it was a new fashion for fur collars. "Belle writes that they're all the rage." The head with its pointed nose and beady eyes stared back at me.

The woman came and went, saying little. "She thinks she's too good to live in a rooming house," my mother said.

Sometimes after I had gone to bed, I heard the woman and her husband climbing the stairs to their room. Occasionally, she sounded giggly and full of fun. Other times she was whiney like Nancy wanting something. From the tone of the man's voice, his wife was not going to get what she wanted.

One Saturday morning in a game with Nancy, I was caught hiding in the cupboard beneath the stairway landing as the couple left the house. The man was saying, "Get yourself a job if you're so bored."

"I tried waitressing. Remember? You didn't like all those men shining up to me."

"You need a respectable job." His foot came down heavily on the landing above my head.

"I can't exactly teach school, now can I? I barely finished school myself."

"What about one of those dress shops on the square? You spend enough time there." He closed the door behind them.

I snuck out of my hiding place to watch them walk to his coupe parked in front of the house. They were still arguing. The man opened the car door for his wife. She sank down in the seat and kept her face turned to the window as they drove away.

My favorite roomer was Miss Nickel who lived at the top of the stairs. She was a fan of the evening radio shows. When I thought I could get away with it, I dried our supper dishes with a few quick swipes so I could sit outside Miss Nickel's door to listen.

"Come on in, child." Miss Nickel stood in the doorway of her room.

"Mom says I'm not to be a bother."

"And you won't be." She patted my shoulder as I squeezed past her. Miss Nickel was rather short and what my mother called plump. I liked the softness of her, comfortable as a feather pillow.

A dark green blind over the room's small window shut out the night, while a lamp next to her rocking chair dimly revealed a narrow cupboard filled with pretty dishes. The odor of onions, probably coming from the covered pot on the small gas stove, hung in the cramped room.

"You're just in time to listen to Kate Smith with me. You climb up on the bed. I'm not ready to give up my easy chair."

The single bed was pushed against the opposite wall. A bank of pillows in various shapes and colors formed a backrest.

"I had to move the bed away from the window, now that winter is taking hold."

My mother always cringed at the scraping sounds of Miss Nickel moving furniture around in her room. "She'll be cutting right through the floor pretty soon, and it'll all fall in on us."

Miss Nickel shoved a stack of magazines and a sewing basket away from the bed's middle. "Scramble up there now." She settled herself in her rocking chair. Reaching across the table she used for eating, sewing, and writing letters, she turned up the volume on the radio.

"Enough of that news. Terrible things going on over in Europe. Ah, here's Ted Collins, Miss Smith's announcer. He sounds like such a nice man, doesn't he?"

I nodded but did not care whether he was nice or not. I just wanted to hear the music. Evidently, Miss Nickel liked the music too. When the first notes rang through the room, she sighed and leaned back in her chair. She stayed in that position while Kate Smith sang. Daring not to make a sound, I nestled myself against the cushions and studied the designs Miss Nickel had sewn on them, using pieces of cloth in bright pinks, purple, crayon orange, and green. She called it something like "apple kay" work.

The announcer came on again, selling something. Miss Nickel stirred. "I always wanted to be a singer. Had great dreams of going away to school and studying, but Mama thought she needed me at home. Of course, I didn't have the figure or face to be a fancy star. But look at Kate Smith...."

"I thought you was a teacher," I said.

"'*Were*' child, 'I thought you were a teacher.' Yes, I was. Still am, I guess." She laughed and paused before going on. "My teaching was mostly reading and writing. Tried a singing class once, but when I wanted to move the children beyond *She'll Be Coming Around the Mountain,* I lost them. One father came to me and said, 'I'm not sending my young'un to school for no singing.'"

"I used to sing with my dad. He went around singing all the time." I turned away and fiddled with the fringe of a pillow.

"Your mama has a piano downstairs. I haven't heard her play it."

"She doesn't play it now that we moved. She says she doesn't want to bother the roomers."

"Maybe that's it. It'd be wonderful to have a piano." Miss Nickel leaned back, closing her eyes, as Kate Smith sang *When the Moon Comes Over the Mountain.* Her cushiony breasts rose and fell above the mound of her stomach. I thought maybe she had gone to sleep.

When the song finished, she righted herself. "But I'll always have my nickel, won't I? My five cents' worth."

I laughed. It was an old joke between us.

"I've been thinking," she said. "Come spring, I'll put the bed catty-wampus across that corner. Maybe get myself a nice fern to put by the window."

Chapter Thirteen

MILK

I feel a twinge of guilt when I remember stealing milk from Larry who was just a baby, but I told myself it wasn't fair for him to have all the milk. Another month had gone by, and still nothing seemed right since my mother moved us into town. Now winter bore down. On those cold mornings, I scrunched in bed next to sleeping Nancy. I couldn't sleep. Fearsome noises moved from room to room in this strange, big yellow house. I waited for the creaking sound of Frankie's cot in the next room. He grumbled as he got up to go out to deliver his newspapers.

His grumbling was different from the fall day he had bounded into the kitchen, a yellow newspaper bag slung over his shoulder, boasting he had a job.

"You said I needed a job," he said to my mother. "Well, I went right down to the newspaper office—that big office full of white-shirted guys pecking away at typewriters—and asked for a job. There was this big guy shuffling papers and chewing on a cigarette. He asked me if I could get up early—guess he didn't know anything about milking cows or doing chores. Anyway, he wanted to know if I could get up early, rain or shine, to deliver thirty papers. I said sure I could. He went on talking, but he was a little hard to understand, with his tongue tangled around that cigarette. Guess he was saying something about collecting money each week and counting out the correct change."

I didn't think Frankie knew anything about doing that and said so. My mother said, "He can learn."

But she had to help him with the money part. She made him dump the tickets and money on the table and count it before turning it into the office. Those coins and bills looked like a lot to me, but when he divided his pile from the one for the newspaper, his was pretty small—especially if there were "skinflints" who didn't pay on time. So he grumbled now about having to crawl out of bed to deliver papers.

Only after hearing the thud of the back door did I peal myself out of the warm bed and slide my bare feet to the cold wood floor. Holding my breath that the heavy double doors wouldn't squeak and give me away, I pushed through to what my mother called the dining room. By this particular morning, I had learned to pick my way around the jumble of boxes mixed in with furniture that hadn't found a proper place in the room yet. Lying on the twisted covers of Frankie's bed was a torn newspaper. Above a picture of people bunched together in front of the Centerville courthouse, large black letters said something about 100 jobs being lost and people crowding into the Relief Office.

The linoleum floor of the kitchen felt even colder to my feet, but I breathed a little easier seeing my mother was not yet at the kerosene range. She was probably feeding the coal furnace in the basement or cleaning the roomers' bathroom upstairs.

I pulled open the back door. The bottle of milk was still there, its surface beaded with moisture. I knew I should leave it alone. On the farm one thing we always had was milk. Now, instead of the blue crock in the center of our table, there was one bottle. My mother said we had to save the milk for Larry. "You're big girls," she said to Nancy and me. "You don't need it like the baby." She would pour out a little for our morning oatmeal, save some for cooking, but the rest was for him.

Stepping out on the back stoop, frost stinging my feet, I didn't feel like a big girl. I snatched up the bottle, gripped it by the neck, eased up the stiff paper tab, and took a few quick sips. Cold milk washed over my tongue, filling my mouth with its creamy taste. It was so good, better than the "blue john" we had on the farm. That's what my father called milk with the cream skimmed off.

I had to have more. No one would ever notice so little milk was gone. After another quick swig, I swiped my mouth with the sleeve of my nightgown, recapped the milk and carried it into the kitchen.

"Child, what are you doing outside?"

I nearly dropped the bottle. My mother stood at the sink washing her hands in a small pan of water. Her eyes went to my feet.

"Whatever's the matter with you? You'll catch your death of cold. That's all I need, a sick kid on my hands."

Although shadows still hung over the kitchen cabinets beside the single window, the electric light bulb dangled unlit from the ceiling. My mother was always fussing about lights being left on. She dried her hands and used the towel to brush something off her dress. "'Bout all that's left down there in the coal cellar is dust," she muttered. She gave up as specks became streaks, filled another pot with water, and dropped two scant handfuls of oatmeal into it.

"What gets you up so early, anyway? It's Saturday."

"You know." I gulped. "Dad's coming today." His visits were a touchy subject since she had taken it into her head to move us into town, leaving him on the farm.

"He would be coming today." She wiped back a dark wing of wavy hair and turned to jab a match against the rough stove grid. A spark flared and spread fingers of flame across the hissing gas.

"Get yourself dressed. Then you can give Larry his breakfast." I started to the bedroom, but she called after me, "Your grandparents are coming today too. Probably before I get any straightening up done." Then under her breath, "Guess Mother will get her chance to say, 'I told you so.'"

"'I told you so' what, Mom?"

"Never mind. There's Larry awake. Get some clothes on."

We hadn't been back to my grandmother's house since that day she and my grandfather brought us to Centerville. I missed going to her house. There everything had a place. The sun came in and the breakfast dishes and furniture shone. Flowered rugs would be warm to my bare feet from one room to another, rooms where I could explore and create my own playhouses. Not like this house with strangers living behind closed doors. When Nancy and I sneaked upstairs to play in the hallways, renters opened their doors to yell at us, "Don't you brats know how to be quiet?"

I complained to my mother, "Why do they have to live in our house, anyway?"

"So we can eat," she said. It didn't seem to be helping much. Eating hadn't been that good, as far as I was concerned. Mostly green beans she had canned and brought from her garden on the farm.

At noontime, before Nancy and I rushed outside to meet our father, my mother made sure we had our faces washed and the parts straight in our hair. We waited behind the yellow house scuffing our feet in the loose red shale that covered the alley. Shivering in the light wind, Nancy clutched her coat over a missing button. I pulled up my limp knee socks and curled my fingers away from a hole in my mitten. Finally his truck rumbled into the alley. Traces of drying manure and tufts of animal hair clung to the stock rack that swayed over the empty truck bed. I figured he had already delivered a load of cattle to the sale barn outside of town.

"Here's my pretty girls." He looked the way he was supposed to— smiling blue eyes, felt hat and suede jacket brushed clean over a uniform-type pressed shirt and pants. Other farmers came to town dressed in overalls they wore every day. Not my father. Once-plush upholstery was rough against our bare legs as we clambered up on the seat beside him. Frankie loved to talk about how our father had cut down an old Buick sedan to make this truck. I had no idea how he could have done that.

Nancy jabbered about our new school, saying she had her own room with other first graders. She didn't have to be in the same room with me anymore the way we were in country school. "It's a big brick building. So big, Ruth Ann got us lost the first day."

"I didn't get us lost."

"Did too. You took us to the highest-up floor. We supposed to be on the first floor."

"I was looking for my room." I turned to my father. "From the top floor there's a spiral fire escape we can slide down at recess time. It's too high and scary for little kids like Nancy. She'd be scared of getting stuck in there."

"Wouldn't either. You think you're so much."

Beneath his wide-brimmed hat, one of his eyebrows went up, like it did when he was ready to laugh.

I had no time for dumb Nancy. "I'm in the B row. A lot of kids are in the C or D row. There are even two boys and a girl in the F row. They can't do anything right. And guess what? I get free milk."

His full black eyebrows moved together. "How come?"

"'Cause I help hand out milk to the other kids." I had gone hot all over when I learned other kids had money for milk and I didn't. Miss Shaw had told me I could work for it. My job was to go into the narrow hall behind the blackboard, take the cool, moist bottles from the wire rack, and place them on the desks of the other children. I didn't tell my father that I drank my milk in the hallway where I could hear the other kids talking and laughing. I didn't really mind because the milk tasted so good.

"Well, whadyaknow, my big girl has herself a job."

"Frankie has hisself a job too," said Nancy.

"How's Frankie doing?" he asked.

I jumped in before Nancy could say anything. "He's got himself a paper route, but he has to give most of the money to Mom. His high school is clear on the other side of the square. He says no one talks about Bruce there."

My father went quiet and soon he pulled up to a little café with a blue neon sign in the window reading *MABEL'S DINER*. Signs in red said "Good Eats" and "Cigarettes." Before we got to the door, I smelled hamburgers frying. It had been so long since I had a hamburger my whole mouth was hungry. Inside the diner smells of pork chops sizzling on the grill and potatoes steaming reminded me of those good eats we used to have at my grandmother's house. No green beans. And there were yummy looking cakes and pies, cut and waiting in the glass cases on the counter.

Sitting on silver-banded red stools at the counter, two farmers in stiff overalls talked in loud voices. "Roosevelt's going to have us in war if he's not careful," one said, grinding his cigarette in an ashtray.

"Maybe that'll get him off our backs, telling us what to do," said the other. He set down his coffee cup and turned to my father. "You bringing pigs into market now, instead of us having to kill and bury them? I hear tell old Max Rhodes killed his pigs all right, but he butchered them for meat. You suppose the Feds will come after him?"

"I don't know about that," my father said. "But I had a good load this morning. Farmer said he might as well try to get something out of them."

We had no more than sat down in one of the straight-backed booths when a waitress, her lips bright with lipstick, hurried up to us. She wore a frilly apron and what appeared to be a flower, but it was really a pink handkerchief folded in some fancy way.

"So these are your girls, Dan," the woman said as if she had heard about us before. "They sure didn't get your blue eyes."

My father laughed. "That's what makes them so good looking, Shirley."

I didn't speak up for a hamburger, so Shirley brought us plates of mashed potatoes and beef spread over two slices of bread. Gravy covered it all. I hadn't seen such a big slice of meat for ages. My grandmother brought us home-canned beef once in a while, but I didn't like it much.

We dug into the food, taking large bites. As usual Nancy made a mess of things, gravy on her face and dripping down on her dress. My mother would be mad. I slowed down when the waitress came back to lean against the booth and talk to my father. She kept standing there talking and laughing in a high laugh that filled the room. The men at the counter turned to watch. I didn't like the way they were grinning, so I said to him, "Mom says to tell you we need more coal."

He took another bite and chewed for a while. "Didn't I just bring her a load?"

"The roomers are always complaining about not enough heat. She says we need more."

"Well, okay, tell her I'll bring her some next week."

Shirley laughed and shook her head. "Poor Dan."

On the way back to the house, my father and Nancy sang *She'll Be Coming Around the Mountain*. Nancy started being silly and shouting out "Choo! Choo!" I looked out the window as we drove past the courthouse in the center of the square. It was easier to see the clock tower now that the elm trees had lost their leaves, but I was more interested in the Woolworth's and McClellan's stores across from the courthouse.

"Could we stop at the dime stores?" I asked.

"Yeah, Dad, could we, pul-ease?" Nancy was good at begging, and he was good at ignoring it.

"Sorry, kids, I have another load to pick up. Don't you get enough of dime stores, living here?"

"Mom doesn't let us go anymore," I said, "not like she used to."

~ ~ ~

Living in town was not as fun as I thought it would be. The big, yellow house was not like Aunt Belle's, not even with those tall double doors leading to different rooms. Doors off the dining room led to an ordinary bedroom, but those off the living room opened to a parlor-like bedroom with large windows overlooking the street. In the living room, a wooden staircase led from the first floor to the second. Best of all was the bathroom off the back stairs. Not even my grandparents had a bathroom. I didn't have to use the farm outhouse where spiders lurked in a tattered Sears catalog, nor could Nancy pester me to go with her because she was afraid of falling down the hole. There was another bathroom upstairs along with three bedrooms.

But those doors were closed to us when renters moved in. My mother said it was too bad doors couldn't shut out the sounds of radios playing or people tramping overhead. More than the sounds, she fussed about bathroom odors that she couldn't seem to get ahead of.

Winter came on, and she forgot about noise and odors and fussed about bills. As they piled up, she rented out the front downstairs bedroom where she and Larry had slept. That crowded her and Larry into the middle bedroom with Nancy and me. The new renter, another salesman, was never around when I was awake. I wondered if he ever used the bathroom.

~ ~ ~

When my father took Nancy and me back to the house, we found the old black Nash parked in the alley. We gave him a quick good-bye and ran inside. From the back hall, I overheard my mother saying, "You might as well know. I have to move. The landlord says I've got too many people in the house."

Nancy zipped forward to see our grandparents. I hung back in the doorway, trying to figure out what was going on. In the baggy dark suit he wore for church and trips to town, my grandfather perched on a kitchen chair that was too small for his big, bony body. Larry sat astride one knee. My grandmother, still wearing her Sunday hat over her crimped gray hair, stepped forward as if to block our path, but I saw the glint of tears in my mother's eyes. They stopped talking, their mouths tight with words we weren't supposed to hear. My grandfather turned to Nancy and lifted her onto his other knee. I expected grandmother's usual questions about school and stuff, but she turned to dig a book out of her handbag. "I brought this for Larry. Ruth Ann, why don't you and Nancy take him into the other room and read it to him?" I wanted to stay to listen, but I knew the talking was done until we were out of the room.

On the other side of the door, we settled on the floor with the book. My grandmother's high-pitched voice carried over my reading. "Like I've said before, I don't know what you were thinking of—packing up and moving out like that."

My mother said, "I thought you of all people would understand. You sure never had anything good to say about Dan."

"And with good reason. Setting you up on that farm and him losing it. We'da been took under too, if your dad here hadn't...."

My grandfather's voice was like the way he moved, slow and easy. "We don't need to go into that."

My mother said, "We paid plenty for that, moving from one rented farm to another."

"We paid too," my grandmother said.

My grandfather cleared his throat.

"Dan lost interest," my mother said. "He'd keep a cow or two for milk. That's all. Nothing extra to sell. Sometimes I'd think he didn't care if that old tractor broke down. He'd rather tinker with it than plant corn in someone else's field."

"No use being stiff-necked proud," my grandmother said. "He had young'uns to feed."

I lost my place in my reading. I loved her, but I wished she didn't take on so about my father.

"I couldn't face another winter cooped up in that cold house," my mother said. "Trying to keep the kids from getting sick. Having to carry in all our water.... Even with the range going full blast, the kitchen was always cold so we spent most of our time in the front room, huddled around the pot belly stove. Last winter was the worst of all. You remember that big snow storm. I was stuck there with the kids. Dan was out in his truck someplace. Drifts so deep he couldn't get home. We still had to carry in fuel. Don't know what I'd have done without Frankie helping me keep the fire going."

Sometimes when Frankie wasn't around, I'd gotten stuck with that job. With wind and snow howling around me, it seemed a mile out to the windmill. One time I forgot my mittens and my hands nearly stuck to the pump. Then there was the trip back to the house, slipping and sliding on snowy ground while trying not to spill water from my pail.

My mother didn't go on to tell about the real scary thing that happened during that snow storm, but I remembered it. To fool us into thinking the chilly front room of the farm house was really warm, she always brought in the kitchen tea kettle and kept it steaming atop the stove. Carrying it back, she must have missed the step going down into the kitchen. I heard the thud of her body and the crash of the kettle against the floor. Mostly, I remember her screams as hot water splashed her leg. She struggled to right herself, her screams directed at us. "Keep back. Keep back."

What happened next is mixed up in my head, except for one thing: the blister that grew above my mother's ankle, like the white of an egg bubbling in a hot skillet.

Nancy poked me to read again. I stumbled on the words while trying to listen to my grandmother's voice. "Well, you've lost everything you worked for, girl. After you moved out, Dan got in that truck of his and drove away."

"Now, Mother," said my grandfather.

"He drove off and left all his corn standing in the field. Didn't even pick it, did he, Dad?"

"That's what I heard."

"Why did he have to do that?" My mother sounded like she was about to cry. "Why couldn't he come with me?"

"Did you really expect him to?" he asked. "In town, Dan would be like a race horse locked in a barn."

"He's living in town now, isn't he?" my grandmother asked. "Living with his sister."

Larry, bored with me starting and stopping to read, crawled away to find Nancy who hid behind a box. My mother was talking, but I had to lean my head against the door to hear her.

"There were other reasons. You know that. You heard the gossip at church about Dan and that woman, same as me." Nobody said anything, and her voice came again: "I thought we could make it, renting out rooms. Belle does it. But everything—the electricity, the water, the coal—they all cost so much. Last fall I made apple butter and sent the girls out to sell it door to door. I think they sold two jars. Nancy said people were mean to them. I won't try that again."

I didn't want to think about that. People peered at us from behind half opened doors, looking us up and down. I closed the book and crawled to a pile of boxes to join Larry and Nancy in their game of hide and seek.

Chapter Fourteen

PIECES

As my grandmother put on her coat to leave, she didn't give me that old tired out warning to be a good girl. In a hurry to get out to their car, she pulled me against the rough wool of her coat for a quick hug and kiss. Her damp cheek surprised me.

My grandfather lingered in the open doorway letting cold air into the kitchen. "I don't know what to tell you, Sarah." He turned his Sunday hat in his hands. "Let us know what you figure to do. I reckon the landlord will still let you use his phone, won't he? Get in touch somehow. Me and Stu will help any way we can."

My mother didn't say anything after they left. I went back to playing with Nancy and Larry in the adjoining room. Beyond the open door, my mother sank down at the table and seemed to go off somewhere in her mind before finally rising to wash and dry coffee cups. She opened the cupboard and lifted the cups to put them away, but the cups went wobbly in her hands. She set them back on the counter, turned away, leaving the cupboard open, and walked into the room where we were.

We didn't have a living room, she had said once—just a "lived-in" room. With one knee, she pushed Frankie's cot back against the wall, smoothed his pillow, and dropped down on the bed, wrinkling the covers again. Her hands fell open in her lap.

"It's all going to pieces," she said.

I didn't know what to say to that. Her dark eyes swept the unkempt room. Crammed with things like our grown-out-of clothes and her church dresses, boxes were pushed against walls to free space for renters who had taken over our bedrooms. Her gaze caught on the chandelier that spun rainbows on the ceiling above where a dining table should have been.

"It's not like Aunt Belle's house anymore," I said.

Her eyes jerked to me. "No, it's not. Can't seem to get away from living in one room, can we?"

She got up from the cot and walked to a box topped with last week's wash. She folded the pieces of clothing and put them into the box and moved to the front room, which now served as an entry hall for the roomers. Only her upright piano claimed any family ownership. Bleak light from bare windows picked out scratches on the piano's black surface. Crowded against the staircase, it looked lonely and a little naked too without family pictures on the top.

My mother had not played once since moving into this house, but now she ran her fingers over the piano lid, leaving trails in the dust. She reached into one of the boxes, took out a sheet of music, and lifted the piano lid. The sounds were harsh with heavy bass notes, not like the melodic songs I remembered her playing. The pounding quickened, grew louder. Larry and Nancy stopped their game as the music rose and crashed around them. Larry let out a whimper. Whether my mother heard him or not, her hands moved more slowly, the music calmer, the strokes letting the treble notes come through. I was glad when the music softened and flowed to a quiet end.

Over the next couple of weeks, Nancy and I went to school as usual until my mother announced she had found another house on the other side of town. Although we had moved several times, I didn't know or think much about the details. We simply woke up in one place and went to bed in another. Nor did I give much thought to the roomers. The people who lived behind the doors didn't really belong in our house anyway. I had just tried to stay out of their way so they wouldn't yell at me or give me some kind of job to do.

That didn't count Miss Nickel. I liked her and the cozy clutter of her room where she let me listen to the radio with her. I supposed Miss Nickel would come with us.

"I can't move with you, dear," the little plump woman told me, surveying the books, pretty plates, and handiwork stacked on her bed. She picked up her quilt blocks, piece by piece, and spread them carefully in a box. "Your mom was hoping I would, but your other place is too far for an old lady like me to walk to the post office, the doctor's office, or even the grocery store." She took a breath. "I'll miss you children. I liked seeing you running about. I'll miss this room too."

Holding a quilt block in her hands, Miss Nickel moved to her corner window. "From here, I can see all the way to the square."

I stood beside her, and we gazed at the green peaks and ridges of the courthouse roof and the clock tower standing above the trees on the snow bound square. Even from this distance I could read the time. The clock faced every direction, and I wondered if we would be able to see it from our new place.

"Makes me feel a part of things," she continued. "I was looking forward to spring when the trees would be leafed out. I'd still be able to see the clock above them. And they light it at night, you know. I thought it'd be like looking at a grand light house across a sea of green."

Miss Nickel walked back to the bed and pressed the seams of the quilt block open with her fingers. "I have an old cousin—she's ailing a bit. She lives on the other side of the square—over by the Ritz Theatre. She says I can move in with her. She'll keep me busy, I imagine. Doubt I'll have much time for my piecework or dreaming about light houses."

Mr. Hamlin also complained that the other house would be too far from the post office. He asked Frankie to find a special box to pack his scrap books in. He grumbled to my mother that he would never have taken the room if he had known he would just get settled and have to move again.

The salesman and his wife who had occupied the other upstairs room packed their bags and left early one morning before my mother got up. "They didn't pay," she said.

Chapter Fifteen

THE "D" ROW

It seemed but days later that Uncle Stu arrived in his truck to move us to the other house. Aunt Violet didn't come along to help. My mother said that wasn't surprising. Violet was usually busy doing something with her church friends. Following Uncle Stu around as he toted boxes, I listened to him mutter about our moving into a section near the levee.

"That's not an area to be living in," he said. "It's all beer parlors and rundown stores along the loading docks. Nobody lives down there but poor whites, the coloreds, and Italians—them that works in the button factory or the coal mines south of town."

"Well, we're going to be living down there," said my mother. "So I guess it's a proper enough place."

It sounded worse and worse to me. Days before I'd been surprised to spy my father leaving our house as Nancy came home from school. I don't know if he even noticed us. He was talking to Mother through the door. "You want to keep on with this? This town living ain't working out so good for you, has it? And I'm stuck at Sophie's."

"How you doing with all that praying and preaching?" My mother gave a harsh laugh. "Moving in with her was your doing. You didn't have to leave the farm."

"Didn't I? I come home one day to an empty house. You and the kids gone. You expect me to go on living there?" He paused. "So you're moving down to the levee now?"

"You got a better place?"

"Probably nothing good enough for you," he said and left without speaking to us.

I wanted to ask my mother why we couldn't move back home, but I could tell she wasn't in any mood for questions.

The new narrow two-story house showed a tired face, chipped with once-upon-a-time white paint. Two small upstairs rooms ducked under sloped ceilings that hung low over the bed where Nancy and I were to sleep. The worst thing about the move was having to change schools again—not that I had any tell-anything-to friends at the first school.

Our walk to the new school took us along broken sidewalks to a bridge that curved upward over the railroad tracks. Half fearing and half wishing for a train to pass beneath us, I gave in to the urge to hang over the bridge rails. Probably the bridge would shake as the train rumbled along—maybe so much that the bridge would fall. Maybe the smoke would sting my eyes, blinding me so I didn't know where I was. My earlier fascination with trains was still with me. I wanted to run along those tracks flung down like a ladder, spanning the shallow gorge on the way to some unknown place. They narrowed into ribbons skirting white banks of snow, and finally into lines disappearing into the grayness where snow and sky became one.

In the other direction, where cinders pocked the snow, the tracks branched out near the depot and led to the round house and the embankment beyond. Frankie had bragged about climbing up there and watching the trains turn around.

I jerked back to reality when I noticed Nancy balancing herself on her stomach, leaning far over the rails. Teach her right to fall, but I would be the one to get in trouble so I yanked her back, and we hurried on across the bridge.

The street leading past the depot and storefronts reminded me of a Roy Rogers movie I had once seen on a Saturday afternoon. I gripped Nancy's hand and wished we could tiptoe past workmen who lounged against loading wagons as they waited for the train. The men kept their hands plunged in pockets of their bulky jackets, but their eyes slid over me before retreating beneath their billed caps.

About a block beyond the railroad crossing stood a little Italian grocery store. I liked to go into the store in the afternoons, even if I didn't have pennies to spend, just to look at the different kinds of candy. Often mornings or afternoons, older school boys poured out of the store, ducked around to the side of the building, and smoked their cigarettes. Above their hands cupping a light, they stared at me, daring me to tell. They knew I'd be too scared. These were the same boys who later at recess squatted in corners of the playground while others made a game of kicking old cans and bottles found along the fence.

That first morning at our new school, I left Nancy with her teacher and scurried off, fearing I would be late to class. Taking the stairs to the second floor, I dodged boys and girls going up and down. I found my classroom, only to be blocked by a cluster of girls standing in the doorway. The girl in the middle of the group spun around so that her pleated skirt flared out above her knees.

"Oh, it's so cute," cooed one of the girls.

"You're so lucky," said another. "My mother never buys me anything."

The girls went quiet as I squeezed past. Smothering giggles, they followed me into the classroom and took their seats. I had to wait at the front of the room for the teacher to seat me. When the girls' hands went to their mouths, covering their whispers, I knew my dress was all wrong. Cut down from one of my mother's church dresses, the dark crepe fabric stuck out like a weed among their cottons and soft wools.

Finally the teacher turned to me. "Another transfer." She meant another nuisance. "We'll start you in this row."

A quick glance across the rows of chin-up, well-combed heads in the first row to the careless sprawl of boys on the far side told me the teacher pointed to the "D" row.

"But Mrs. Shaw put me in the "B" row," I protested.

"I'm not Mrs. Shaw, am I?" Right then, Mrs. Graham changed into Miz Grim.

I sank into the assigned seat next to a boy who looked older and bigger than the other boys. What really surprised me were the two dark-skinned boys in the end row sitting there quietly with their heads down. I had seen Black people on Centerville streets. I remembered my grandmother saying they were like anyone else, but I had never seen them in stores or church—unless they came to perform as singers. Certainly, I had never seen them in school. Across the aisle from me in the "C" row, the only Black girl in the class turned to me and smiled.

Mrs. Graham was a small woman with a pouty mouth. She didn't like me. "Let's see how well you can do." She ordered me to the board to work out problems in fractions and long division. I did not do well. The other kids watched as I erased and started over, erased and started over. Later during history class as Mrs. Graham scolded first one student and another—even the girl in the twirly dress—for not remembering the date when America was discovered or the names of some ships, I decided Miz Grim didn't like anyone.

Going home wasn't much better. The house was cold. My mother wore a heavy sweater and a pair of Frankie's socks pulled over her own most of the time. There were no treats after school, but she fixed supper early—usually beans or potatoes with a bit of meat stirred in.

A man who wore a suit and carried a small sample case rented one of the upstairs rooms. He took a long time in the bathroom in the mornings while Nancy and I waited outside, shifting from one foot to another. I did not like his eyes. From under pinkish, swollen lids, they moved over me, making me feel like I had no clothes on. After my mother found him hanging around outside the door when Nancy was taking a nap, she told him to pack his bags and get out. For days, her sign "Room for Rent" hung in the front window. No one came.

The only fun person at school was Ruby, the girl who sat across from me. We both liked to sing, but Mrs. Graham ruined that for us. During singing class her thin voice led us through the same line over and over. Ruby started out good and strong, but then her voice faded and dropped out.

During recess we sat next to the schoolhouse on a patch of sidewalk warmed by the sun. I tucked my legs under me and stared out at a group of girls pushing and laughing with each other near the swings. Ruby was silent. Then she sang in a high-pitched voice. It was the song Miz Grim had tried to teach us. I laughed. Ruby's voice went up a notch.

"Now, children," I mimicked, "we need to try that again."

Together, we squeaked out high and exaggerated notes until giggles doubled us over. The girls at the swings turned to look at us. Ruby and I leaned our heads against the schoolhouse wall, letting our laughter dribble away.

"Why don't you come home with me after school?" Ruby asked. "I got some new paper dolls."

For a minute, I couldn't answer. Finally I said, "I'll have to ask my mother."

"Maybe tomorrow?" Ruby prompted.

"I'll see."

I asked my mother if I could go home with Ruby the next day after school. She seemed pleased that I had a friend but asked, "Where does she live?"

I couldn't tell her what section of town Ruby lived in. "Just a couple of blocks north of the school, I guess."

"You'll have to walk Nancy home first. And you can't stay too long—maybe an hour."

The next afternoon, I took Nancy within sight of our door and ran to meet Ruby who waited at the corner.

We followed the street for two blocks before turning to an area I had never been before. I figured we were on the other side of the Round House. The street dropped off into lanes covered with red shale. Houses were smaller here, some never painted. Dogs lurked under porches. Beside some of the houses, rusted-out cars sat on rims. At other houses, overalls swung from the clotheslines. We laughed at the frozen legs rounded out like stovepipes.

"The men who live there work in the coal mines, like my dad," Ruby offered.

Ruby's house was also unpainted, but there were lacy curtains in the two front windows and the porch was swept clean. When we entered the house, Ruby's mother, who looked just like Ruby, hesitated a moment over her ironing board. Studying me, she returned the flatiron to the stove before greeting me and giving her daughter a hug. I was surprised to see a man sitting at the table, a cup of coffee in his hands. His skin was dark as coal. Ruby ran to give him a kiss.

"This is Ruth Ann," she said. "She sits next to me in school."

"I made some cookies today. Each of you can have a couple." Ruby's mother placed a plate of cookies on the table. "I'll fix you some cocoa too."

Ruby sat down on one of the chairs at the table. She motioned for me to take the other chair. I couldn't take my eyes off her father. He smiled and pushed the plate of cookies to me. I sat down.

"Now, let's see, Ruby," he said. "What have you been doing today?"

From the coat Ruby had hung behind the door, she took out some folded papers and spread them before him on the table.

One was a spelling paper, a 100% at the top.

"That's good, Ruby girl. That's real good," her father said.

I ducked my head. I had misspelled two words on my test. Ruby's other papers were for arithmetic. Three problems were circled with big red check marks beside them.

"Looks like you're having a little trouble here," her father said. "Bet your mama can help you with these. You talk to her after supper, okay?"

Ruby's mother glanced at the papers and turned to the range, sliding the handle from the iron she had been using to another one heating on the stove. She lifted the iron and tested it, like my mother did, by licking her finger and touching it to the base of the iron. There was a little hissing sound. From a basket of dampened and rolled clothes, she shook out a white shirt and pressed her iron to it, filling the air with the scent of starched cotton. Several other white shirts hung from a hook on the wall.

"Those are the banker's shirts," said Ruby. "His wife brings them every Monday."

After our cookies and cocoa, Ruby opened the door to her parents' room and took me inside to get her new book of paper dolls. The room was small, dark and cold, furnished only with a dresser and an iron bed covered with a crazy quilt comforter. Another quilt covered the window. There was another tiny windowless room, about the size of a pantry, for her older brother, Ruby said. There was no bathroom. I had seen an outhouse in the back yard.

Ruby's "room" was the cot pushed into a corner of the main room where her drawings decorated the walls. As we sat cross-legged on the pink chenille bedspread, Ruby opened an older book of paper dolls between us. Most of the dolls and dresses had been cut out. The faces of these dolls were pale and white. The faces in the new book looked like Ruby.

"My uncle sent me these from Chicago," she said.

I took one of the older dolls in my hands, holding it so the head wouldn't fall backward. I chose one of the cut-out dresses and folded the tabs over the doll's shoulders while Ruby pressed one of the new dolls out of the other book. She worked carefully so as not to tear them. We exchanged dolls and outfits, dressing them to go to the movies, shopping, or church.

"Of course, I have to go to my church," I said, "and you go to your church. Let's dress to go to the movies."

"I have to sit in the balcony," said Ruby.

"Why?" I asked.

Ruby lifted one shoulder in an "I-don't-know" shrug. I lifted an eyebrow and shrugged too.

Ruby's father rose from the table and took a long, heavy coat from the rack behind the door. As he pulled a cap over his ears, Ruby explained he had another job, taking care of the passenger cars at the railroad yard. I supposed she meant cleaning them.

In no time at all, Ruby's mother pointed to the clock. Ruby walked with me to where paved streets and sidewalks began. We waved good-bye to each other, and I skipped on home.

Chapter Sixteen

SOMETHING RED

My mother had a job sewing at the hospital. What she would sew at a hospital she didn't know, but she guessed she would find out. Anyway she could take Larry with her to work.

Aunt Belle mailed one of her coats for my mother to wear on the mile walk to the hospital. Coming from Aunt Belle, the coat was surprisingly plain, black with no fur collar or fancy buttons. My mother said it wasn't as heavy as she would have liked. She shortened the sleeves but decided to leave the skirt long. Warmer that way, she said.

Mornings became a rush: My mother getting our breakfast, little as it was; packing a sandwich with half an apple in our old country school dinner pails for me and Nancy—we couldn't come home for lunch since she wouldn't be there; barking out orders for Frankie to bank the furnace before he left for school—no need for it to be roaring away with no one home. In her hurry, she sometimes forgot to check if Nancy and I had our books, tablets, mittens, or galoshes before we left for school.

My mother would barely be out of her coat and Larry down for his nap when we came home from school, and the house wouldn't have warmed up yet. Although we kept the doors off the kitchen and main room closed to retain heat, cold air leaked in the window near my mother's rocking chair and ran along the wood floor.

After bringing her first paycheck home, she said maybe things would work out after all. That was different from what she had been saying since moving us into "this gray, beat-down house," as she called it. She had never before had her own paycheck, and she was ready to celebrate—buy something to warm up the place a little.

Besides, she needed a break after a couple of weeks bent over a sewing machine. She asked if I wanted to go shopping with her. Did I want to go!?! Not Nancy! Me!

When we first started out to town, my mother fussed about leaving Nancy and Larry behind. She wasn't sure Frankie would watch them carefully enough. I could have told her something about that, but then we wouldn't go shopping.

It was one of those bright winter mornings that made my cheeks tingle. She quickened her step, swinging the long coat around her legs. Even her hair had a bounce to it, and her cheeks were rosy as she lifted her head to the tree limbs still tinged with frost against the sky.

"Did you ever see such a blue?" She spread her gloved fingers across her purse, like the money inside gave her some kind of freedom. "We'll have ourselves a special day."

Sidewalks along the square were still pretty quiet. A man in a suit smiled at my mother before he crossed over to the courthouse. She turned away, but a little grin grew on her face. I wanted to go to one of the dime stores on the facing street, but she went into Underwood's Furniture Store.

This was a place I didn't even like walking past, because Mr. Underwood's store was also the funeral parlor. Back when we lived on Washburn Street, I had gone uptown with Miss Nickel, and we stopped by Underwood's to look in the front window. Not to see the furniture but the casket displayed there. I had tried not to think about the dead body closed inside it. Miss Nickel was interested in how many flowers there were. If there were so many flowers we could hardly see the casket, she declared the dead person must have been someone really important—or rich.

Miss Nickel had said, "My life has been tolerable, but my nickel's worth won't put many flowers in Mr. Underwood's window."

I was glad there wasn't a casket in the window that day as I followed my mother into the deserted store. Breathing in scents of new fabric and furniture wax, we waited amidst rows of sofas, chairs, dining sets, and bedsteads. Finally Mr. Underwood, the undertaker, came out from the back room. Tall and thin, he stepped between aisles of furniture, his long pale fingers touching oak tables and velvet chairs. I wondered what else those fingers had touched.

Clasping his hands in front of him, he bent in almost a bow to my mother. "And what may I do for you, Madam?"

"I'm looking for an area rug," my mother said. "Something bright."

He led us to the back where rugs lay in stacks. I kept my eye on the door to the back room.

My mother quickly spotted a dark red rug. Mr. Underwood rolled back other rugs so she could see how a vine of gold roses ran across the red background. She knelt and brushed her hand across the thick tufts, then turned over the price tag. "It's more expensive than I expected."

The undertaker man waved those long, thin fingers saying something about a down payment and installment plans. "Just a little each month."

She stood up. "I'll have to think about it."

He nodded like he knew my mother could never buy such a rug.

Outside on the street, she stood for a moment, cars circling the square and people hurrying in and out of shops. "Let's try the White Swan. I'm not ready to go back to that house yet."

The White Swan! I'd heard the starched girls at school talk about eating at the White Swan with their parents after church on Sundays: how they wore their best dresses, gloves, and patent leather shoes to sit at tables covered with white table cloths.

When I said that at the supper table, Frankie had laughed. "You mean the 'Dirty Duck?'" He went on about how the town kids would load up their convertibles and take off during noon hour for cokes and hamburgers there. He'd heard it was quite the place after the evening picture show. Kids sneaking in stuff. They were the ones who called it the "Dirty Duck."

On the other side of the front window stood a couple of tables with white cloths and pretty bowls—a little like those I had seen at Aunt Belle's house.

As we entered, a waitress stepped forward to meet us. "It's a little early for lunch." She led us to the booths and wood tables at the back where several men sat drinking coffee.

With a sweep of her long coat, my mother turned to a table at the window. "This will be lovely."

The waitress glanced back at the man at the cash register before offering us menus.

"That's all right," my mother said. "I'll have coffee—with cream please, and a hot cocoa for my daughter. And, oh yes, two of those little cakes I see on the counter."

The waitress left us, and we tugged off our coats.

The pretty dish that centered the white cloth was really a bowl filled with small white cubes.

"It's sugar," my mother said.

I reached for one, but she pointed to some silver pincher-like things. "Use the tongs. But take only one. Those are probably for the luncheon ladies when they have their tea."

"Are we luncheon ladies?"

"No." She grinned and said in a loud whisper, "but don't tell the waitress."

I couldn't remember when she had last acted like this. Did money do that?

"Are you going to buy the red rug?" I asked.

"It was real pretty, wasn't it?"

The waitress came back and set plates of cake and heavy mugs before us.

"It would warm up the place." said my mother. "It'd be nice for Larry. He's always crawling around." She stirred cream in her coffee. "Awfully expensive, though."

"But you got your check."

"That check won't cover much." She drank from her cup. "I don't know…." She stared out the window. "Probably not." She set down her cup and picked up her fork. "Let's enjoy our cake. You have to have real cream to make frosting like this."

I had to use both hands to lift my cocoa. It was yummy and didn't burn my tongue like hot cocoa sometimes did. I wanted to put another sugar cube in it, but my mother shook her head. I sat up good and straight. It was special to be there in the White Swan Café, looking out at people on the street. On the opposite corner across the broad square, the Ritz Theater stood proud with its orange tile roof.

"That's where Miss Nickel lives," I said, pointing.

"Somewhere over there?" my mother said.

"She said the Ritz Theater."

"Did she?" She seemed to be counting pennies in her head and drank the last of her coffee. "We better be getting home. I'll go pay while you finish your cake."

"But the rug…"

"It's too expensive."

I scraped frosting from my plate and picked up crumbs from the cloth.

Our coats on, we had just stepped outside the café door when my father's truck came down the street. "Look, there's Dad." I rushed out to the sidewalk, but he had gone on by. A red hat showed through the back window, worn by some woman sitting next to him.

"Who's that with Dad?"

My mother had not moved from the doorway, but stood watching the truck disappear down a side street.

"Maybe it was Aunt Sophie," I said, but I couldn't imagine Aunt Sophie wearing a red hat.

With a jerk, my mother spun around. "Come on. We're going to buy a rug."

Chapter Seventeen

RELIEF

I was surprised to find my mother all dressed up before breakfast. I wanted to ask where she was going or if company was coming, but she had been touchy since losing her sewing job at the hospital a few days before—something about them not wanting her to bring baby Larry to work. Watching her rush around, red-faced and frazzled-looking while Larry yelled his head off, I knew better than to ask questions.

There was no real breakfast—just a glass of water and some runny oatmeal. Nancy sat beside me, dipping her spoon in and out of her cereal.

"I want some milk," Nancy said.

"I'm sorry, honey." My mother jostled Larry up and down in her arms. He still howled. "There isn't any."

Nancy shoved the bowl away from her.

"Eat it, Nancy," my mother said. "That's all there is."

"I don't like it."

My mother pushed the bowl back to Nancy and turned to spoon oatmeal into Larry's mouth.

Frankie bounded down the stairs, still tucking his shirt in his pants. His eyes swept the table. "Nothing to eat. I'm late anyway." He headed for the door.

"Wait, Frankie, I need you to help me today."

"Aw, Mom, me and some guys got plans over the noon hour."

I'd heard Frankie talking with his new friends, Sam and Buck, about noontime being "cruising time." They had stopped by the house once—back when my mother was working and Frankie was supposed to be watching us kids. Buck talked big about how they should hitch a ride with one of the roadster guys and get in on some cruising.

"Them that has roadsters ain't gonna bother with us," Frankie had said. "They just want to pick up girls and head for the café on the square."

"More likely to the city park," laughed Sam.

"Well, there's always some guy with a clunker," offered Buck.

"I ain't interested in waiting around with my tongue hanging out," Frankie said. "Forget going to the square. Whyn't we hike down to the levee?"

I guess that's what Frankie meant when he said to our mother, "Us guys're aiming to go down to the garage. They got a new '40 Chevy in."

"There's no point of your dreaming about a new car—or any other kind of a car," she said. "I have to go down to the courthouse, and it'll probably take most of the day. It's too far for me to carry Larry all the way, so I need your help."

"I'll get in trouble if I don't go to school," Frankie said.

"I'll send a note with you tomorrow."

"A note ain't likely to soften up that scowly lady in the principal's office," Frankie said.

I couldn't believe Frankie was scared of any old principal. Must be something else up. Maybe I should offer to go to the courthouse. Then I'd get stuck with watching Larry. I'd rather play with Ruby.

Fixing to leave as soon as Nancy and I were out the door, my mother pushed beaded combs into her dark hair to keep it from falling across her face. An old hat she had perked up with bits of veil and faded ribbon lay on the table in easy reach. It was like she was getting ready for church.

At school Miz Grim kept me in at recess to work on my fractions, and I didn't get to play with Ruby. I should've gone to the courthouse with my mother. Back when we drove in from the farm, Nancy and I went to the courthouse often, usually to wait in the women's lounge while my mother finished her shopping. But I liked walking through that broad hall, hearing my shoes ring out on the marble floor, climbing the wide staircase to look out windows that rose high over the stores along the square.

I forgot about Miz Grim and Ruby when Nancy and I came home to the strange quiet of the kitchen. My mother sat at the table with hands folded, Frankie in the rocker picking at his guitar, Larry on the floor chewing a cracker. I forgot about them too, when I saw the table.

It was loaded with grocery sacks full of food. Nancy and I dug through, pulling out bacon, hamburger, flour, eggs, milk, sugar, potatoes, dried beans, cheese, a box of oatmeal, and one small bunch of over-ripe bananas.

"Is all this for supper, Mom?" Nancy asked.

I couldn't remember ever seeing so much food. "Where... where'd it come from?"

My mother just sat there, still wearing the dress from that morning. The blue silk material didn't look pretty anymore. It looked old and used, like the made-over dress I'd had to wear that first day in a new school. Frankie picked at the guitar strings—pling, pling, pling. I realized only the crackers had been opened. Nothing cooked on the stove.

My mother's words came from deep in her throat. "All those people down at the courthouse—I never saw such people... so poor. Now, I'm one of them."

"But all this food, Mom," I said. "It's great!"

Frankie jumped up from his chair, sending it rocking back and forth. "Stupid, you don't know what you're talking about." He jerked open the door to the unheated front room and headed for the stairs.

"I'm not either stupid." I went after him, past the dusty piano and unpacked boxes.

"You're a dumb-ass kid." He pounded up the stairs.

"Mom, Frankie's talking dirty."

She didn't even look up. "Close the door, Ruth Ann."

I whirled to close the door and tore up the stairs after Frankie. "I'm no... what you said."

"Well, you're a dumb something. Where do you think that food came from?"

With a narrow window overlooking the alley clogged with sooty snow and a ceiling that hunched over the bed, his room was like the one where Nancy and I slept. But his room had no floor register to let heat up from below.

"Maybe Dad brought the food," I said.

"Dad! Ha! No, it's from Relief." He ducked under the ceiling to sit on the bed.

"Relief?" That couldn't be. Only poor people went on Relief.

"And Mom made me go to that courthouse with her. At least Sam and Buck didn't see me following along, toting my kid brother," Frankie said.

"I been to the courthouse lots of times. It's kinda like a castle in a fairy tale."

"You are a dumb kid. This was no fairy tale. You shoulda seen the crowd lined up, waiting in the cold. All kinds of folks. Even the guy from my history class. He'll probably blab it around school—me being there."

"You didn't have to wait outside, did you?" I wondered if Ruby had to go on Relief, would she have to wait in the cold with the others? I drew my knees up and covered them with my skirt.

"Oh, we got to go first. It wasn't much better inside." He pulled his guitar across his lap. "I didn't know what we were doing crowded in with those people stinking up the place. One guy kept going on about the coal mine being closed. 'Fifteen years,' he kept saying. 'Fifteen years. Fifteen years I worked in that mine.' Most of the men didn't say much, just shuffled along in line, smoking their cigarettes and throwing them down to mash under their feet. One poor guy came along to mop away the slush melting from our dirty boots. He was plenty careful not to let that mop touch anyone's shoes."

"Mom squished in with all those people?" I couldn't believe it.

"She was there all right, along with them other folk that work in the factory." Frankie's voice took on an edge. "Those guys giving her the eye. Her in her silly hat—she stood all the straighter, holding Larry like he wasn't even heavy. Those other women—with their headscarves mashing their hair—they all looked alike. Soon as they got a chance, they slumped down on the benches. Not Mom. She stayed on her feet."

He plunked a couple of strings on his guitar. I thought he was done talking, but something pulled him back there again. "I didn't know what we were doing there. Not 'till the line made it to the lobby, and we stood under those big windows where everyone could see us…" Frankie shook his head again. "It was some woman, sitting on the stairs with a whiney baby, saying, 'We could've got along, you know… but after the factory closed…. Never in a million years did I think we'd come to this—going on Relief.'"

He fairly spit out the words. "That word hit me like a ball bat. The line pushed us forward. The woman said again, 'Never in a million years did I think we'd have to go on Relief.'"

"Relief is really bad, huh?" I'd heard snooty girls at school making fun of another girl, whispering about her being on Relief.

"It was bad going into that office. Mom handed Larry to me while a starched-collared guy pushed his glasses high on his red nose to look down on us. That little pipsqueak had the nerve to say to me, 'You're a big, husky boy. Why aren't you working at some job?' Bet he never crawled out of bed at dawn to deliver newspapers. Mom told him I had to go to school. Real snippy like, the man said, 'He's not in school today, is he?' Mom spoke up again saying she'd tried to get a job. The collar guy came right back at her, 'Then you'd take a job from some other poor sap.' There I stood in that place, Larry squirming in my arms, and that guy kept pushing his glasses up and down on his nose, shooting questions: How many kids did Mom have? Why was she living in town when Dad was on the farm? Was she divorced?"

"Divorced?" I was shocked. "They're not divorced."

"Mom and Dad ain't exactly together, either." Frankie went back there again. "Finally the guy wrote out a check for Mom. He told her, 'This'll help you buy some food for your kids. You'll have to wait until next month for the full allowance.' Mom pushed the check deep in her purse, like it was gold. We headed for the door, but the jerk took another jab at us, calling out to Mom, 'Best you go back to the farm.'

"You shoulda seen Mom's head go up. She turned on her heel and marched out of there, and that veil atop her hat stood up like a sail. I took a good hold on Larry and kept up with her the best I could."

My brother went quiet, his fingers picking out a chord on his guitar. It was out of tune.

Outside the window, it was getting dark, making the room darker and colder. I shivered.

"Frankie, are we poor?"

He gave me a funny look. "I never thought so." He stood the guitar against the wall, shoved the music books to the floor, and flopped face down on his cot, pulling a blanket up over his head. "Beat it, will ya?"

Downstairs, I found my mother emptying the sacks, putting food in the cupboard. I didn't want any of that "Relief" food, but I was hungry. "Mom, you want me to peel some potatoes?"

Chapter Eighteen

FOOD

"Okay, do what you want," my mother said, finally giving in to my begging to spend a weekend with my father. On his visit the previous Saturday, he had mentioned his family's plans to get together for my grandmother Lou's birthday. I saw a chance for me to get away from home for a while.

"Can I come too?" I had asked him.

"You'll have to ask your mom."

I never knew whether my mother would yell at me over the least little thing or sit rocking with Larry in her lap, not caring one way or another. Her acting like that went back to the day Nancy and I got home from school to find Relief food on the table.

Ever since, I didn't know what to expect at school, either. When I heard girls tittering behind their hands, I wondered if they knew about The Relief or maybe about my going to Ruby's house. One day in class, Ruby had edged a paper doll out of her pocket and whispered, "Meet me at the swings." I nodded in agreement, and during recess we pulled our swings together to examine the doll.

"My uncle sent me another book of dolls," Ruby said. "You want to come to my house to play?"

Before I could answer, a couple of the starched and pressed girls had sidled up behind us. "Hey, look," said one, "a colored paper doll. Oh, I guess it's not a real colored doll. Look at her hair."

The doll's hair was long, black and shiny, not tightly curled like Ruby's.

"They just colored in a white girl's face," said one of the starched girls. "Who'd want that? It's ruined."

"Yeah, you start playing with a doll like that, the color might rub off," said the other girl.

"Then you could go down to the courthouse and line up with those other coloreds," laughed the first girl. They both laughed and grabbed the other swings.

They did know about my mother and Frankie going for the Relief!

Ruby was waiting for my answer. "You wanna come?"

"I have to go right home," I said. "My mom's sick."

Ruby put the doll back in her pocket. Looking over at the starched girls, she let go of her swing and moved to the schoolhouse wall. After a while, she just sat down on the ground.

Going off with my father meant I wouldn't have to think about any of this. It had taken a couple of days of working on my mother for permission, but finally it was Saturday and I waited in the driveway for him to pick me up. Nancy stood in the doorway, whining like usual. I stuck my chin up as we drove away.

The thing I had not figured on was staying overnight at Aunt Sophie's house. My father had stuck around barely long enough to eat supper and went off to work at some garage. After an evening of playing board games with my cousin Mikey—games he always won— it was bedtime. On this dark, wintry night, the little bedroom off Aunt Sophie's kitchen seemed different than it had that time after the Jamboree, the narrow bed lonely standing so high on its iron bedstead. My aunt pulled back the covers, and I jumped a little to get into the bed.

"I made this comforter myself," said Aunt Sophie, tucking it under my chin with her *Fels-Naptha* scented hands. "Collected the wool scraps and stitched them together." The stitches reminded me of bird tracks in the snow, and the coverlet smelled like old coats left in a closet. It was so heavy I could barely move.

Aunt Sophie stood at the foot of the bed, her back as straight as a poker. In her black dress, she blended into the dark of the room, her pale face blurring into white hair. With her hand on the oil lamp, she asked, "You going to be okay?"

I nodded, but I wasn't so sure. "Say your prayers, and you'll be okay." Aunt Sophie blew into the lamp. With a gasp of smoke, the light flickered and died. As the door clicked behind her, I shrank into the feather bed. I mouthed the words, "Now I lay me down to sleep. If I should die...." I twisted in the bed, trying to make a place for my head in the feather pillow. It fought back, billowing around me. A feather quill poked my cheek.

The room was so dark. There was nothing in the room but me on this high bed that creaked with my every move. I almost wished Nancy was here with me, even if she did hog the covers.

I closed my eyes and tried the prayer again: "If I should die…. If I should die…." My eyes popped open and fastened on a glimmer of moonlight swaying like a tall pale ghost in the window. Another block-shaped ghost with dark curving arms crouched against the wall. I squeezed my eyes tight and scrunched deeper into the bed. The heavy comforter held me down. Sucked in by the musty smell of mattress and feather pillows, I felt nearly swallowed.

Gradually the warmth of the bed overtook me, and the ghosts faded. One retreated into the narrow-curtained window. Another fled into the mirror on the dresser. My eyes darted from one to the other to make sure they did not become ghosts again. I tried the prayer again, rushing past the "if I should die" part.

"Time to get up, girl." Had I gone to sleep? Maybe the ghosts had come back after all. I opened my eyes to darkness and pulled covers over my head. The voice came again. It was Uncle Josh. "Come on, girl. We gotta get on our way."

I heard Aunt Sophie say, "This is crazy, Josh. The beans aren't done. They'll need three or four more hours."

"They can finish cooking at your mother's house."

"You'll have to wake up, Ruth Ann. Your uncle says we have to go."

I pushed back the covers. Aunt Sophie stood in the kitchen doorway, dimly lit by a single electric bulb dangling from the ceiling. I stumbled out to the kitchen and sat down at the table.

"Josh, it's the middle of the night," Aunt Sophie said. "The children have to have something to eat."

"Woman, we ain't taking time for no sit-down breakfast. That city slicker beat me to this birthday doings the last two years. Not this time, he ain't. Cut the young'uns off a chunk of bread. I'll take one too."

My cousin Mikey appeared, still pulling on his overalls. "Son," his father said, "get yourself dressed proper. Then jerk that pot of beans off the stove and put them in the back seat of the car."

"Josh, what's Mama going to say—me bringing beans hard as rocks?"

"Like I said, boy. Soon as you're dressed, take those beans out to the car."

I had no idea what was happening. I was supposed to be going to my grandmother Lou's birthday dinner with my father, but he had gone on ahead and I was stuck at Aunt Sophie's house with Uncle Josh and cousin Mikey. Nancy was at home, still snug in our bed, and I was up in the middle of the night because Uncle Josh was acting like he was in some kind of race.

Aunt Sophie and I were still changing into our Sunday-go-to-meeting clothes—except we were skipping meeting that day—when we heard Uncle Josh start the car. He revved up the motor like he'd go off and leave us. Mikey rushed to take the pot of beans to the car. Aunt Sophie grabbed an old quilt, an armload of newspapers and followed her beans out the door. I was right behind her, finding my way through the drizzly, cold dark.

I supposed the quilt was for us to wrap up in, but instead Aunt Sophie wound it around the pot of beans, already covered with newspapers. She was still busy tucking the quilt around the pot when Uncle Josh jerked the car into gear and backed out the driveway. Gravel spun from under our wheels as we rounded the corner to Main Street. A cat turned yellow eyes on us and high tailed it in the opposite direction.

There had been no talk about Mikey driving this time. Uncle Josh was in too much of a hurry. Large in his heavy coat, he took up most of the front seat leaving Mikey sitting close to the door. Out on the pavement we passed farm houses, their windows still dark. No one was up yet. We whizzed along. "We got a good start," my uncle said. "That city slicker Stout ain't going to beat us. Him and his fancy new Oldsmobile."

Mikey was ready for the race. "Uncle Stout has beat us every year. But not this year! Huh? Pa?"

"Not this year." The car went faster.

Beside me in the back seat, Aunt Sophie leaned forward to press newspapers more tightly around the pot of beans.

Drizzle no longer clouded the wind shield and the curve of hills appeared against a gray sky. Recent rains had washed away most of the snow, but yellowed clumps like beards of old men still clung to ditches. We were nearing the last stretch, a dirt road that was bound to be muddy. Soon after the first sharp turn onto the unpaved road, we saw a farmer carrying a lighted lantern and a milk bucket walking to his barn. He stopped to look at us. With a shake of his head and wave of his hand, he disappeared into the barn.

Off the highway, the beams of Uncle Josh's headlights spun across the road ahead of us. Fat rolls of mud marked deep ruts cut into the rain-soaked surface. From stories my father told, I knew my uncle wasn't about to let a little thing like mud stop him. We jolted along, sliding in and out of ruts. The lid on top of the beans jiggled as mud pelted the underside of the car's fenders.

Clattering over the boards of a bridge, Uncle Josh gave the car more gas for the hill ahead of us. In the front seat, Mikey leaned forward as if to give us more power. "You think Uncle Stout's Oldsmobile can make this hill, Pa?"

"He drives in from a different direction," said my uncle. The climb became steeper and Uncle Josh geared down. The pot of beans slid to Aunt Sophie's feet. She pulled back the quilt to press newspapers against the pot.

We crested the hill and were on the way down, speeding to fence posts that marked the sharp turn at the bottom. Uncle Josh braked at the last minute, sending the car into a skid to the ditch. The lid on the bean pot went flying off, striking the door while soupy sauce splattered across crumpled newspapers, the quilt, and Aunt Sophie's skirt.

"Josh, the beans," she cried.

Uncle Josh was busy dodging fence posts and getting the car back on the road. The rear wheels whirred on a patch of snow. Finally inching forward, they took hold on firmer ground, and we were on our way again. The road now took a straight line to my grandmother Lou's farm. Mud spun away from our wheels.

"Nothing to stop us, now, huh Pa?" asked Mikey. Aunt Sophie dabbed at tomato sauce spotting her skirt.

As we topped a rise above my grandmother's farm, the sun broke through the haze to lighten the dull tan of her smallish two-story house. Suddenly Uncle Josh hit the brakes. Mikey slammed against the dash board and I bounced against the back of the front seat then back again. Crash, went the pot of beans against the front seat. The lid flew off. The pot rocked back and forth, tipping to Aunt Sophie. Beans and sauce spilled over her feet.

There gleaming in the morning sun in my grandmother's driveway was a new Oldsmobile. Uncle Stout leaned against it, a wide grin on his face. Uncle Josh pounded the steering wheel. "He beat us!"

"Oh beans!" The way Aunt Sophie spat out those words told me she didn't care about any old stupid race. Mikey and I kept our mouths shut.

A little afraid of what Uncle Josh might do next, I concentrated on the scene before me: Uncle Stout's car between us and my grandmother's house, lights dim in her kitchen windows, laughter ringing out as my father stepped out on the porch to see that Uncle Josh had been beaten again.

Finally our car crept forward to stop beside the Oldsmobile. Uncle Josh and Mikey sheepishly stepped out of the car to face Uncle Stout and my father's glee. After some handshaking and back slapping, I figured they were friends again. I wasn't so sure about Aunt Sophie. With bean sauce still staining her skirt, she picked up her nearly empty pot and walked past the men like they weren't worth even a glance. I followed.

My grandmother Lou was different from my other grandmother. My mother's mother was a tall no-joking-around woman. In her kitchen everyone knew she was the boss. My grandmother Lou, short and round, was having a second cup of coffee while waiting for the aunts to come and take over. When she leaned forward to give me a hug, I wondered what kept that great pile of white hair atop her head.

"Child," she said, "you're thin as a rail. We need to get some meat on those bones."

After leaving my coat in her unheated bedroom, I found two of my cousins, Barbara and Laverne, huddling near the potbelly stove in the living room. They griped about their father, Uncle Stout, making them leave home so early. But that didn't stop them from boasting about beating us. We fiddled around with my grandmother's pump organ for a while, but I was drawn to the kitchen where it was warm from the fire in the wood range and steamy with the smell of food, including what was left of Aunt Sophie's beans bubbling on the stove.

In short order other relatives arrived, and soon half a dozen women crowded the kitchen, preparing dinner. I vaguely remembered my father's other sisters, Aunt Vivian and Aunt Verdie. I supposed I was related to the others in some way, but I could never keep them straight.

My aunts gave me hugs while I sneaked looks at the food being prepared, especially the large pot of beef and broth.

"You hungry, honey?" asked Aunt Verdie, who gathered up narrow strips of homemade noodles drying on a floured tea towel and dropped them into the pot of beef.

In the bubbling broth, noodles rose and fell, becoming thicker and flecked with bits of beef. I breathed in the steam, letting the meaty smell sharpen my hunger. Near me, Aunt Vivian mashed potatoes, great mounds fluffy with milk and butter. A couple of women—aunts by marriage or maybe distant cousins—conferred over the gravy, then checked biscuits in the oven and pronounced them almost done. It was time to call in the men.

Uncles and cousins tramped in. Coats, hats, and gloves were dropped onto a small bench beside the door only to slip unheeded to the floor. My father and his look-alike brothers, Vern, Virgil, and Vinnie, plus others considered "grown-ups," found places at the large oval table in the kitchen.

"It is my birthday," my grandmother reminded them and seated herself at the head of the table.

Shunted off to sit with the younger kids at a table in the living room, I kept my eyes on my aunts, standing near the kitchen range and ready to serve. I almost groaned out loud when my grandmother asked Aunt Sophie to say grace. I bowed my head but peeked at Barbara and Laverne. Like good girls, they closed their eyes and folded their hands in their laps. A couple of the boys rolled their eyes. Mikey's eyes were squinched shut. As Aunt Sophie's voice rolled up hills and down into valleys, I thought of buttery potatoes and hot biscuits.

"Oh, Lord, we just pray...." Aunt Sophie's voice was going higher and higher when I felt a sharp kick on my leg. I would have kicked back, but I didn't know where to aim. I peeked at two of the boys. They seemed too bored to move. Mikey's grin did not quite match his tightly closed eyes.

Before long around the big table, one chair after another creaked under the restless weight of hungry men. I hoped Uncle Josh didn't have to pray too. Whether he wanted to or not, he didn't get a chance. As soon as Aunt Sophie said, "Amen," Uncle Vern jumped in, "A-men! Those biscuits smell mighty good."

Aunts scurried to move food from the range to the tables, and a plate was placed before me. At last, I could eat.

After seconds or maybe thirds, the boys disappeared, probably to the barn. Feeling stuffed after several helpings of mashed potatoes and gravy, I followed Barbara and Laverne into my grandmother's bedroom where they sat on a rag rug playing with their dolls. Smoothing the flouncy skirt of her china doll, Laverne asked me, "Where's your mom? Why didn't she come?"

"Shh," hissed Barbara. "We're not supposed to talk about her. She ran away, remember?"

"She didn't run away," I said.

"My mother said she did." Barbara picked up a doll in a jumper that matched her own.

"Well, she didn't. She's home with Larry and Nancy."

Barbara bent her doll forward. It cried.

My uncles scraped their chairs back from the table and then the plink, plunk of guitars tuning as they gathered in the living room. Who wanted to play with silly dolls anyway? I went into the living room and sat down on the floor near the potbelly stove.

"You get enough to eat, Ruthie?" asked my father. He nodded as I did. Leaning back in his chair, he said, "Yes, sir, a good meal and a warm fire. What more can a man want?"

"I thought you might be wanting more." Uncle Stout grinned.

"Not from stories I been hearing," laughed Uncle Vinnie, my father's youngest brother.

"A person's liable to hear all kinds of things," said my father. He turned to Uncle Josh, who had been stoking the stove with wood and now warmed his backside. "Set yerself down, Josh, and stop hogging the heat. I got a true story that'll warm you up.

"You remember Hank Heisel, don't 'cha?" my father asked. The uncles rested their guitars against their legs, their laughter already bubbling. "You know, I bought my threshing rig from him? This happened a few summers ago on a sizzling hot day. We was using Hank's Fordson tractor and binder to cut grain…"

"Stout here," interrupted Uncle Vern, "probably don't know what a binder is."

"It's a machine that cuts a swath of oats, runs them up a canvas, ties them in bundles and spits them out on the field." My father said it in a voice that implied anyone should know.

"Right," said Uncle Stout.

"Anyway, at noon time, we went in to eat dinner, and then come out to finish the oat cutting, with me on the binder and Hank on the tractor. That tractor had a cast iron seat, and after setting in the sun while we was eating, it was hot enough to fry eggs and maybe a strip or two of bacon. We put a hay bundle on it to give Hank some protection.

"Now, Hank was hard of hearing, could barely hear it thunder. So we rigged up a way of communicating. We tied a long piece of binder twine to the suspenders of his overalls and run it back and tied it to the binder. That way, I could signal him if something went wrong. You know Hank Heisel... his machines was held together with baling wire and chewing tobacco. Anyway, Hank was driving the tractor along at a good clip when the pin come out of the binder's draw bar." My father turned to Uncle Stout. "That's what connects the binder to the tractor. Well, the pin come out. The binder stopped. Hank and the tractor kept going, but the twine gave a yank on Hank's overalls, jerking both him and the bundle off the tractor. There was Hank flat on his back in the oat field, his overalls still tied to the binder, and his tractor was running off without him. He jumped up. All excited, he decided the quickest way to catch that tractor was to get loose of them overalls. So, lickety split, he skinned out of his overalls. Only thing was... he wasn't wearing anything underneath!"

"Is this true?" asked Aunt Verdie, who had been hovering in the doorway. The uncles waved her back into the kitchen, and my father went on with his story.

"So here is Hank naked as a jaybird running faster than blazes, streaking after the tractor. 'Bout up to it, he took a flying leap. Landed smack dab on that hot iron seat! The second time he ran after the tractor..."

The uncles were laughing so hard I didn't hear what happened next.

Uncle Vinnie said, "I hardly knew Hank Heisel, but everyone said he was the most level-headed fellow around, so level-headed that tobacco juice ran out both corners of his mouth."

My grandmother appeared in the doorway. "Sounds like it's about time for some singing." The uncles pulled their guitars across their laps. Uncle Virgil strummed his guitar idly while my grandmother settled herself at the pump organ. She pulled out stops and pumped the pedals with her feet. Sound whooshed from the pedals as her fingers fumbled through different chords. She turned to me. "We need your momma here to play." Some looks went to my father.

Her hands finally lit on the right keys, and she pounded out the melody of *In the Evening by the Moonlight*. Guitars and singers followed. She motioned for me to sing along with her. We went from song to song—"Just Molly and me and baby makes three. We're happy in my blue heaven," to *My Wild Irish Rose*. I liked the sound of "K-K-Katie, beautiful Katie." Before long, Aunt Sophie left the dishes to the other women and joined us. We switched to songs I remembered from church when we had lived on the farm. The words were sad, but when my father and uncles' voices came together in what they called harmony, they looked happy. And they all smiled when my father's voice went really low or when Uncle Virgil's went high.

The music broke off when the boy cousins came back to the house, tramping their feet on the porch but still tracking bits of straw into the kitchen. Their faces bright with cold, they searched for any food that might be left out for them, but their mothers shooed them away, saying it was time to go home.

I grabbed my coat and ran to my father's truck. I didn't want to ride back with Uncle Josh. My grandmother and father were behind me. "That child is looking downright peaked," I heard her say. "How are the other children?"

"All right, I guess," he said.

"They're growing up without you, Daniel. Larry is walking, I hear, and your boy Frankie—he's almost a man. Can't you fix things?"

"Doesn't seem like it," he said and lifted me into the truck.

Chapter Nineteen

DIVORCE

My father wheeled his truck onto the bumpy gravel behind the house that I was supposed to call home. It was cold and empty. I hadn't noticed before how the back porch sagged away from the house, and it was all gray. If I was coloring a picture, I'd have to use up a whole gray crayon. It would take only a few strokes of black to outline the porch screens, ugly and out of place in winter, and a couple more to separate the roofline from the sky. Maybe I could use a squiggle or two of red and blue to draw the twisted rag rug hanging over the back stoop.

I was surprised when my father followed me onto the porch, tugging the screen closed behind him. He waited beside me, standing on the gritty, winter-tracked floor as I opened the kitchen door. The first thing I saw was my mother in an old print dress and drooping apron, standing at the sink peeling a potato. At the sight of us, she dropped the knife and let the potato roll into the sink. She gave me little notice but took off her apron while keeping her eyes on him. Larry was playing blocks on the red wool rug next to the warmest place in the room, the metal floor register directly above the basement furnace. Nancy sat in my mother's rocker next to the window supposedly folding diapers. As soon as she saw our father, she let out a squeal, dumped the diapers on the floor and went running to him, jumping into his arms.

"Hey, you're getting too big for me." He stumbled as if he might fall over.

"I'm not too big, Daddy." She wound her arms around his neck.

"Stand down here a minute. Let me see how many inches you have grown." Nancy slid to her feet, and he held his hand way above her head. "Must be all of six inches."

My mother pushed her hair back from her forehead. "Life does go on."

"I hear Larry is walking," my father said.

I wanted to help my brother show off his ability to walk, but Nancy beat me to it and was already lifting him to his feet. "He walks funny," she said.

My father grinned as Larry toddled to him. I glanced at my mother. She seemed to hold her breath as Larry wobbled, then plopped down on his diapered bottom. My father laughed and picked Larry up and steadied him to walk again.

Watching Larry take a few steps and fall, take a few steps and fall was old stuff to me, so I turned away to hang my coat on a kitchen chair where my father had dropped his hat. I almost wished I was back in my grandmother's kitchen steaming from pots on the wood range stove, noisy with talk of women as they dodged around each other to prepare food. This room looked like nobody loved it. The only color in the room came from the rug. There was no cozy clutter of newspapers, toys, or books. No pictures on the wall to say we were here to stay.

The round oak table with its pedestal base, good for resting my feet on during meals, took up most of the space in the room. Except for the usual salt and pepper shakers and a half-empty sugar bowl, the table was bare.

Everyone was busy with Larry. "We had all kinds of food to eat at Grandma Lou's house," I said. "Real meat, biscuits, mashed potatoes and chocolate cake."

That got Nancy's attention. "Did you bring me some choc'lit cake?"

"How could I bring you some? And I played dolls with Barbara and LaVerne. They had dolls in pretty dresses, and they could cry…"

"You didn't bring me any cake?" whined Nancy.

"I hear you got some help with groceries," my father said.

"Help?" my mother shot back. "Is that what you call it? I suppose your mother and sisters had some choice words to say about that."

"Well, it's something. All I got is my truck. You figuring on staying here, are you? Now that you got the Relief and all. And your folks are probably helping out."

"I haven't seen Mother and Daddy for over a month."

"Grandma and Grandpa would bring me cake," pouted Nancy.

My father carried Larry back to the red rug, knelt briefly to place some blocks before him, before saying, "Oh, they'll be here—seeing to their little girl, soon as the snow goes and the roads dry up."

"Look Dad," I said. "We have a real bathroom, right here by the kitchen."

"Yeah," said Nancy, grabbing his hand and pulling him to the bathroom. I followed, my sister turning faucets and showing our father that hot water actually came out of one.

"Um-hmm." He nodded and headed back to the kitchen. "Where's Frankie?"

"Out someplace with his friends, I guess." My mother picked up another potato to peel.

"I been hearing things," he said.

"And how would you hear things?"

He turned to me. "Why don't you and Nancy run on upstairs? Your mama and me need to talk."

A flicker crossed my mother's face. "Take Larry with you. Watch him on the stairs."

I looked at my mother. She just nodded for me to leave.

I picked up Larry and shouldered open the door to the unheated front room. Nancy rushed past me to get to the warmer rooms upstairs. Larry was heavy to carry up the stairs. In the room where Nancy and I slept, I put him down on the bed pushed back under the slanted ceiling. I told Nancy to watch him and settled myself down near the metal floor grate that allowed heat to flow upward to our room. I wanted to hear what my parents were talking about.

"There are women who like having a man around," he was saying. "Don't mind cooking his vittles, keeping him warm at night."

Something hit the sink. "I'm sure you've found such a woman. There's always some floozy going after a man, any way she can get him"

"I ain't about to be no easy pickings. But I'm not for this going it alone either. I need a family and a fireside to call my own."

There was no reply from my mother.

"I thought after you had to move down to this part of town and with Frankie up to no good, you'd be ready to call it quits with this life—fancy bathrooms and all." My father paused like he was waiting for an answer, but he went on. "Now, you have outsiders bringing in food. Guess there's no use of me hanging around."

I hung over the register waiting for her to say something, but it was my father who spoke. "Like I said, I need someone and some place to call my own." He paused again. "I reckon divorce is the next step."

The word *divorce* rang out loud in my ears like a bell that kept ringing in the silence that followed. Why didn't my mother say something?

There was the sound of a chair moving, and I could imagine my father clamping on his hat. The kitchen door thudded closed, and the screen door banged. I hurried to the window. Marching along, his arms stiff like he had his fists clenched, my father kicked at a clod of dirty snow. The truck, cranky about starting, made grinding noises. With another growl and a sputter, the engine caught hold. Wheels spun over gravel as he backed into the street and sped away.

Everything went quiet. Larry had fallen asleep on the bed, and Nancy lay beside him playing with her doll. It wasn't supposed to be this quiet while it was still light outside. One of my favorite books from country school was on the floor near the window. I picked it up and sat with it long after the light in the room had dimmed too much for me to make out the words.

Finally my mother called us down to supper. She had her apron on again, and her dark hair had slipped from its combs to hang over her eyes. "We won't wait for Frankie." She ladled soup into bowls and set them on the table. "I can't imagine where he is."

The soup, potato with rings of onion in watery milk, was hot and smelled good, but there was no meat in it. I thought of the beef and noodles at my grandmother's house.

Later, I lay in bed next to Nancy, listening to her breathe. Finally sure she was asleep, I folded back the covers and slipped out of bed. Pulling my flannel nightgown down over my knees, I knelt on the floor and pressed my forehead against the side of the bed.

I closed my eyes tightly and spoke into my folded hands: "Dear God, please don't let my mom and dad get a divorce."

Chapter Twenty

VISIT FROM AUNT BELLE

My father didn't visit the next Saturday, but Aunt Belle and Uncle Lars did. My mother had told us they were coming. She kept rushing around, sweeping and swiping up dust. She made Nancy and me put on our Sunday dresses even though it was only Saturday and we were staying at home. My mother dressed Larry in the only romper suit he had not outgrown before she put on the navy dress she had worn to the courthouse.

As the car drove up—I could tell it wasn't my father because the engine ran quiet and smooth—Larry dirtied his pants so my mother had to take him into the bathroom to clean up.

Nancy and I hurried out to the porch as our aunt and uncle unfolded themselves from their big, black car. Wearing hats and long winter coats that almost swept the sidewalk, they were taller and more grand than I remembered. Clutching her purse and another bag, Aunt Belle kept her eyes on the sidewalk as she stepped carefully in her shiny black patent leather shoes. She held her coat away from the screen and kitchen doors as she walked through. And there they were—inside our kitchen.

The sound of water running came from the bathroom. "Larry grunted in his diaper," Nancy said.

Aunt Belle's nose went up. "I can tell."

The toilet flushed, and my mother called out, "I'll be there in a minute."

Uncle Lars and Aunt Belle didn't bother to reply. They waited tall against the kitchen door. We stood gaping at them. Crowned in their hats, they made me think of a king and queen in one of Nancy's picture books. With a sudden move, Uncle Lars swept off his gray felt hat—the kind my father called a *fee-dora*—mussing up his hair so that it stuck up from pink scalp. Before I could've said *one, two, three*, he dragged a kitchen chair back from the table, took off his coat giving it a couple of quick folds, sat down on the chair, and draped the coat across his knees. The hat went on top of the coat. He leaned against the straight back and said to Aunt Belle, "Do what you came for." It was a little like Frankie letting me know he didn't have time for what he called my foolishness.

Aunt Belle seemed stuck in place, standing there under the turkey-like feather on her hat. I wondered if the feather tickled her forehead when she turned to look around the room. I thought of her house, colored plates and pictures on the walls, chairs too plush to sit on, and saw how poor this room was. Finally with a little shake of her head that made the feather bounce, she lifted the paper bag she had been carrying and placed it on the table. "I brought you something. There's one for Larry too."

Nancy ripped into hers. It was a book of paper dolls. When I opened mine, it took me a minute to figure it out—tiny spools of colored thread, some small scissors, a piece of cloth with needles stuck in it.

Aunt Belle spread the cloth out on the table. "See, there's a pattern for you to embroider."

"Thank you." I ran my fingers over the blue tracings. Then I folded up the material and turned to Nancy as she opened her book.

We heard water running again, and soon my mother came into the kitchen carrying Larry. "I'm sorry. His timing isn't the best."

"I supposed he would be trained by now," Aunt Belle said.

My mother raised an eyebrow, and I remembered her saying, "Belle's never had any children, but she knows just how they should behave." Now she said to me, "Ruth Ann, take Aunt Belle's coat, will you please?"

Aunt Belle laid her coat across my arms, and I carried it into my mother and Larry's bedroom. Beyond the door my mother always kept open to the kitchen heat, I put my face against the coat and breathed in the mixture of mothballs and my aunt's perfume. The fur collar was kitten-soft against my cheeks. Someday, I told myself, I would have a coat that was all fur.

When I came back into the kitchen, Aunt Belle stood on the rug that my mother had bought while she worked at the hospital. With the toe of her shoe, Aunt Belle traced the vine of gold roses that ran across the deep red background. "Nice rug. A lot like Mother's rug."

"Yes, it's wool," my mother said. "Thought it would warm up the room. Please take a chair at the table." She nodded to the closed door to the front room. "It's pretty cold in there, I'm afraid. I made coffee. Would you like some?"

Uncle Lars still held his coat and hat on his lap and didn't budge from his chair. "No thanks. We don't have time."

"But I made some...," she began. The evening last, my mother had counted out nickels and dimes so Frankie could run to the store to buy coffee.

"We are on our way see Mother and Dad," Aunt Belle said as if explaining. "But I would like a cup of coffee." She sat down at the table.

My mother put Larry in his high chair and turned to the coffee brewing in a pan on the stove. Uncle Lars carefully put his hat and coat on another chair and pulled up to the table. I placed cups and saucers before them. Aunt Belle gave Larry his gift. He put it in his mouth and chewed on the paper wrapping. I unwrapped it for him and put the toy car on his tray.

"Ruth Ann, don't you like the sewing kit?" Aunt Belle asked.

"Yeah, it's nice."

"I thought of bringing you some piano sheet music, but I didn't know if your mother was still giving you lessons."

I couldn't remember the last time she had given me a lesson or even sat with me at the piano. "The piano is off in the other room."

Uncle Lars stirred great spoonfuls of sugar into his coffee. He seemed surprised by the coffee grounds that floated to the top. "Didn't any of your renters move with you?"

"No, it's a bit far from the square, and there's no bathroom upstairs."

"Just as well, maybe." He topped off his coffee with milk. "We had to let a couple of our roomers go. They weren't paying their rent."

"Times are hard for everyone," said Aunt Belle. "Lars' patient load has fallen way off. And I have fewer piano students."

"And we still have the payments on the house." Uncle Lars watched Larry run his car back and forth across the high chair tray.

All grown-ups ever talked about was money. I picked up the folded sewing packet and moved to kneel on the rug beside Nancy. Torn bits of paper were scattered on the rug and across the open pages of brightly colored clothes. Nancy was making a mess of her paper dolls. I reached for the book. "Let me cut them out for you."

She swung it away. "I can do it myself."

I sat back on my heels. The grown-ups had their heads together, their voices whispery with secrets. The feather on Aunt Belle's hat dipped as she said to my mother, "This is not going well for you, is it?"

"Not the way I hoped."

"Doesn't Dan help you any?"

"He just says I was the one who moved out."

The feather wagged. "But to go on Relief."

I fiddled with my sewing kit while listening hard. A needle stuck my finger.

"I have kids to feed," my mother said. "If I could've kept the roomers and the house on Washburn Street."

"Women have no business sense about these things," said Uncle Lars. "You need to go back to Dan."

Larry's car bumped over the edge of his tray and clattered against the floor. My mother picked up the car. He dropped it again. She left it there and went to the cupboard to get some crackers.

Uncle Lars rose from his chair and pulled on his overcoat. Aunt Belle's teeth came down on her lip. She opened her purse. "I'm sorry." She passed something to my mother. "We do have the payments on the house."

My mother went into the bedroom to get Aunt Belle's coat. As she handed it to her, I thought my mother was about to cry.

The fur on Aunt Belle's coat tickled my cheek as she bent to kiss me good-bye. "I'll send you some music, Ruth Ann. Then when the weather warms up you and your mother can practice."

The door was closed behind them and they were gone. My mother cleared the table, looking at the leftover coffee in their cups. "She gave me five dollars."

Chapter Twenty-One

FINDING FRANKIE

My mother flipped the curtain back from the window overlooking the side street, let the curtain fall, and went out on the porch to look both ways along the alley. She closed the kitchen door slowly behind her. "Where is that boy?"

Frankie was late coming home from school. That should have been no surprise to my mother. Frankie seldom came home directly after school. In fact, he was often late for supper, especially since the Relief thing. His being late made no sense to me. We now had something to eat at suppertime. Never anything like a whole hamburger that you could smother with pickles, onions and ketchup. You had to hunt for the hamburger in my mother's homemade noodles or the gravy you spooned over mashed potatoes, but at least it didn't leave your tummy crying for more.

My mother crossed to the wool rug and knelt beside Larry where he lay on a pallet next to the floor register. She ran her fingers across his forehead and smoothed back wisps of damp, dark hair. "He's burning up. Ruth Ann, bring me a cold cloth. Wring it out good."

Larry had been whiney before I went to school. Now from across the room, the sandpapery sound of his breath went in and out. I hurried to take her the cloth. It still dripped from the faucet.

Lifting Larry in her arms, my mother settled with him in the rocking chair, and with gentle motions she bathed his forehead. Nancy grasped the arm of the rocker. "Is he sick?"

"Yes, Nancy, he's sick. He needs a doctor. Ruth Ann, if Frankie doesn't come pretty quick, you're going to have to go down to that garage and find him."

Me? To the garage! That was right next to the levee. Nancy and I had to walk near the levee on our way to school. My mother always told us to walk fast and not stop anywhere.

Since winter had set in, Frankie spent some time twanging away at his guitar, but usually he just complained about town living. "There's nothing to do here." After he met Sam and Buck, "going to the garage" seemed to be something to do.

They would stop by sometimes after school to pick up Frankie. I remembered the first time they had shuffled into our kitchen. My mother had given them a good once-over. Sam stood there with his reddish wrists hanging out of his sleeves. Under her look, his chin went up and he jammed his hands into the pockets of his jacket. Buck, a skinny guy, seemed kinda lost in his droopy, brownish coat. He stuck close to Sam.

Later at the supper table, my mother told Frankie she didn't much like his new friends, especially Sam. She had smelled cigarette smoke on him, and if Frankie wanted to live in her house, he better not come in smelling of cigarette smoke. Frankie scooped more gravy on his potatoes. She went on to say she'd noticed a bit of fuzz on Sam's face. "Is he still in school?"

"Mom, I ain't for setting here, cooped up with little kids. At least, down at the garage, Louie lets us do some tinkering—with an old jalopy or maybe a motorcycle."

After that, Sam and Buck waited on the porch for Frankie, except for times that my mother wasn't home and Frankie was supposed to be watching us kids. Then I heard things about a back room where guys played poker. That made me wonder how much time they were spending at the garage.

My mother got up from the rocking chair. "I can't wait any longer. Ruth Ann, wrap up good and go tell Frankie to come home now. I need to get to the doctor's office before it closes. You never know, the doctor might send us to the hospital, and Frankie needs to be here to stay with you girls. "

She pulled my hood forward over my cheeks before I left. "You have your boots on? Okay?" Cradling Larry in her arms, she stood at the door and called out to me. "You'll do fine, Ruth Ann. It's like you were going to school."

The first couple of blocks were just like going to school, including passing the vacant lot this side of the garage. I hated walking past that lot. Someone might be hiding in one of those junked cars or maybe there'd be a hobo looking for a place to sleep. That afternoon, snow covered everything except a stack of tires and the battered top of an old Model A. There were no tracks in the snow.

A couple of cars were parked beside the garage, a low building that stretched back from the street. On the other side of the front square window were several boys. I pushed open the door marked *Louie's Cars and Parts.* They were high school boys, circling and pressing their heads against windows of a shiny, new car. It had to be the '40 Chevy Frankie talked about.

One boy in a suede jacket lifted his head just long enough to bark at me, "Close the door, kid." He sounded like Sam or Frankie, but Frankie was not there.

I tugged on the boy's sleeve. "Have you seen Frankie?"

"Look, brat, I don't know any Frankie. Is he one of the grease guys in back?"

I stepped away from him and went to a door opening onto a dirt floor. This was similar to the shed-like garage I'd been to with my father and Frankie in Littleton: the same greasy smell, the same cars on rims in dusty corners, the same type of men sitting on old chairs or overturned buckets near a pot-belly stove. But no Frankie.

Near a beat-up car on jacks, one guy leaned against a fender watching a man working under the hood. I went up to the working man. "Mister? Louie?"

He lifted his head in surprise, pulled a greasy rag from his pocket and wiped his hands. His stubbly beard was as black as the rag.

"Mister, I'm looking for Frankie. My mom sent me after him."

"Frankie? Girl, I ain't seen him in a while. Used to come in a lot, but those friends of his—Sam and Buck—they ain't interested in what makes cars run. They just want to drive one."

"I gotta find him." I felt like crying. "Larry's sick, and Mom says I gotta find him."

"Now, girlie." He leaned to me. "Don't get yourself upset. Sam and Buck like going to the pool hall. Reckon that's where Frankie's off to."

A guy sitting near the stove spoke up. "Yeah, I seen 'em going there a while ago."

"That's where you'll find him then," said Louie. "You know where that is?"

I nodded. Sure, I knew it was one of those places along the levee, a place Frankie wasn't supposed to be.

The high school boys were no longer hanging around the car in the showroom. Like my father would have said, the car was a dandy. I wanted to run my hands over the shiny chrome and gleaming black metal, stand on the running board to see inside, but my mother had said I was to find Frankie and to find him fast.

Railroad tracks separated the garage from the raised levee. I twisted my head to look both ways, and my hood fell back from my ears. I stepped down across the bed of cinders and railroad ties and clambered up the crumbling concrete steps to the levee. I hurried past the tobacco shop with its Prince Albert signs and dusty display of pipes, past the hardware, past men sitting on the edge of the levee, their legs dangling, their lanterns and dinner pails on the cement walk beside them.

"You lost, girl?" one asked.

I ran, wishing I was off the levee and on the other side of the street. I'd stopped in the little Italian grocery over there for penny candy and seen women with their husbands enter the little café. I remembered my mother saying women had no business on this side of the street.

With my mittened hand, I pawed at my hood trying to pull it back over my ears. Finally there was the pool hall, behind dirty windows covered with advertisements for *Lucky Strike* and *Camels* plus *Red Mountain* chewing tobacco. I couldn't see inside but beyond the door with its peeling green paint, men were talking and laughing.

Pushing open the door, I still couldn't see. Yellowish smoke watered my eyes and tickled my nose. How could Frankie be in this place? I closed the door behind me and stood shivering, not knowing what to do.

A couple of men sat at the bar. Under their railroad-type hats, they squinted through their cigarette smoke, making cracks about the guys at the pool table who took turns circling it. One of the players yelled back, "Quiet, I can't hear myself think." He poked a stick at a yellow ball. I guessed the ball didn't go where he wanted because he let loose some swear words. The railroad guys laughed.

I wanted out of there, but heat from the stove at the center of the room felt good. An old man—a geezer, my father would have called him—sat hunched in a chair there, his whiskery face buried in red long johns poking above the collar of his raggedy coat. A spittoon sat near his feet. I didn't want to go close to him.

At the back of the room a door swung open and a man carried out a tray of something to the bar. Maybe Frankie was in that room. Beyond the open door, some guys sat around a table—playing cards I thought. I'd seen pictures of men like that outside the movie house. 'Course I wasn't allowed to go to those movies, but back when Frankie had his paper route, he went. Edward G. Robinson movies, he called them.

With a brown bottle in hand, a man got up from the table and came to the door. Clenching his cigarette in one side of his mouth, he yelled, "Joe, don'cha know better than leave the door open?" The door shut.

Joe set the tray behind the bar where red-lipped girls smiled down from pictures advertising *Coca Cola* and *Dad's Root Beer*. According to warnings my grandmother gave about pool halls, there might have been other bottles hidden behind the bar. I looked back at the whiskery man just as he leaned forward and shot a yellow stream to the spittoon.

"Jake, can'cha hit that thing?" Joe grabbed a rag and walked to the mess around the spittoon. Then he saw me.

"Wha'cha doing here, kid?" Joe picked up the spittoon. "You looking for somebody?"

Trying not to think about that stinking, slimy thing in his hands, I took a deep breath. "F-F-Frankie?" I croaked. "I'm looking for Frankie."

"Frankie?"

"Mom needs him."

The door to the back room swung open again and a kid came out. It was Sam, laughing before taking a long drink from a brown bottle. Buck was close behind him, and then Frankie. Each held a brown bottle.

"You guys," Joe hissed. "Not out here. You want to get me closed down?"

When Frankie saw me, he looked like he'd been caught stealing chickens, but he still held the bottle.

Sam seemed to think it was a big joke, me being there. "Hey, Frankie, you got company."

I grabbed my brother's hand. "Larry's sick. Frankie, you gotta come."

"After a while," he said, like he was trying to shush me.

"Mom says *now*."

"Ah, Mommie says *now*," Sam jeered.

His eyes going from Buck to Sam, Frankie tried again. "I said later."

"Larry's sick. Mom says you gotta come." I was about to cry.

Buck snickered when Sam said, "See, boy, you gonna make your little sis cry." Sam reached out and took Frankie's bottle. "We'll save this 'till you're growed up some."

"All you guys got some growing to do," Joe said. "Bringing that beer out here."

"Keep your shirt on, Joe," said Sam. "That cop's probably down behind the round house doing his own drinking."

Joe gave him a look.

"Okay, okay," Sam said. "Come on, Buck. Too bad Frankie has to go home to Mommie."

Laughing, Sam and Buck left Frankie and went into the back room.

Outside, Frankie walked fast like he didn't want anything to do with me. I had to run to keep up with him.

Chapter Twenty-Two

THE UNDERTAKER MAN

My mother took off the minute we reached home. She didn't wait for Frankie's answer to her question: "Where were you?" She just wrapped another blanket around Larry and said, "The doctor's office will be closed. I'll have to take him to the hospital emergency room." She was already half-way out the door. "Frankie, you look after the girls like you're supposed to."

She was gone. She didn't even notice the beer on his breath. The evening didn't get much better. Frankie was still mad at me for coming after him. Nancy kept asking when our mother would be home and what there was to eat. There wasn't much—only some bread and butter.

She didn't come home, and she didn't come home. "Was Larry really sick?" Frankie asked like he was getting worried. Finally he said we might as well go to bed. She would be home in the morning. The next morning, Larry was asleep in his bed, and she was waiting for Frankie to come down for breakfast. She didn't ask questions about the day before. Instead she said she needed him to go to the drugstore downtown for some special medicine. "They open at nine o'clock. I want you there waiting for them."

He asked about school.

"This is what we need to do today." She counted money into his hand.

"That's a lot," Frankie said.

"Yes, that's a lot."

Days later, Larry was getting better, but he still needed medicine. Coming home after another draggy day at school, I felt something was off the minute I opened the kitchen door. My mother assured me Larry was okay, but the room seemed more dreary than usual. I yanked open cupboard doors looking for some graham crackers and told my mother how mean ole' Miz Grim had been—scolding me and Ruby. Miz Grim never scolded the starched girls. I didn't bother to mention that she had caught me passing a note to Ruby. We both got in trouble for that. I was already feeling bad about the time Ruby wanted me to go home with her.

It was Nancy who asked, "Where's the rug?"

I realized what was missing. It was as if somebody cozy and friendly had got up and walked out of the room. The rug was gone and so too was its vine of gold flowers that glowed like a circle of warmth. Larry played on a rumpled crazy quilt thrown across the linoleum. I remembered my mother had used the quilt to block the winter draft from one of the windows on the farm.

"Where's my rug?" Nancy asked again. "Where am I going to play with my dolls?"

"I had to sell the rug," my mother said.

"But my dolls liked the rug."

"You can use the table. I had to sell the rug."

Maybe a couple of Saturdays later, my grandparents showed up in their mud-spattered car. My grandfather paused outside the door trying to scrape mud from his buckle overshoes. He gave up and teetered on one foot and then the other to pull them off.

My grandmother burst into the kitchen carrying a basket. "Is Larry all right? Is that why we had to get out on those roads?"

"Larry seems okay, now," my mother said.

"Then what's so fired up important about you calling us? You know what a spring thaw does to our roads. Your father nearly got stuck a couple of times before getting us out to the gravel."

"We made it, Mother." My grandfather was inside, taking off his coat. "Let's hear what the matter is."

"Oh Daddy, I'm in the most awful trouble." And my mother burst out crying like a little kid—worse than Nancy.

One of my father's words jumped into my head—dumbfounded. That's how my grandfather looked, dumbfounded.

My grandmother took off her coat, and instead of hanging it up like she always told us to do, she dropped it on a chair. "Belle told us about the Relief, but what on earth...?"

My grandfather came to himself again. He patted my mother on the shoulder, not quite putting his arm around her. "Now, Pet, come on. Come on, it can't be that bad."

"It is. It's horrible." She cried even harder.

My grandmother motioned to the basket on the table. "Ruth Ann, I brought some cookies, and there's a fruit jar of milk. You can manage that, can't you?"

She turned to my mother. "Come on, Sarah, get a hold of yourself. You're scaring the youn'uns to death." She put her arm around my mother and steered her to the bedroom. My grandfather followed and closed the door.

I lifted Larry into his chair and gave him and Nancy a cookie. The lid on the jar of milk was tight, and I had a hard time unscrewing it. Sounds of my mother's sobbing came through the door. Larry stopped banging his cup against the tray. Nancy picked raisins out of her cookie and lined them up in front of her.

"I sold it," my mother wailed.

"But if it wasn't paid for...?" came my grandmother's voice.

"I had to buy medicine for Larry, and there was the hospital bill. They wouldn't wait."

My grandfather was talking. I couldn't hear his words, but they had that low hum of "It's going to be all right."

My mother was crying and talking again. Her words rode high between sobs. "He said if I don't pay, he'd, he'd send me to jail."

The lid of the fruit jar flew loose, sloshing milk across the table.

"Hush now, child," my grandmother said. "That man's crazy. He can't do that. What store was it anyway?"

My mother murmured something, enough to tell me she was talking about the undertaker's store where we had bought the rug.

My grandmother spoke up, sounding like herself again: "I could have told you not to go to that store. Underwood must not be getting enough dying business."

Their voices rose and fell blurring the words together then quieted with the steady sound of my grandfather: "It's going to be all right." I drank from my glass of milk and took a second cookie. I lost my taste for it when he mentioned my father.

My grandmother said, "You can't expect Sarah to go back to him when he's been fooling around."

"Far as I know," he said. "Dan's still living with his sister Sophie."

"I hear talk," my grandmother said. "That woman's after him."

"He's my husband," my mother said.

It went quiet, and finally they came out of the bedroom. My grandmother shivered and rubbed her forearms. "It's cold in there." She went to stand over the floor register.

They stayed with us for a while, asking again if Larry was better and oh-ing and ah-ing about his walking. Of course, Nancy had to get out her reading book and show off. My grandmother asked me some questions about school. "It's okay," I said.

"I'm sorry to miss Frankie," she said.

"There's a garage down on the levee," my mother said. "He and his friends like to spend time there."

She still didn't know where I had to go to find Frankie that day.

She didn't get to the money talk until my grandparents pulled on their coats, getting ready to leave. "If I had some help with the rent...," my mother said as if she were afraid to ask.

"We'll go down to the store and settle up about the rug," said my grandfather. "That's about all we can do now."

"We don't have cash money coming in," said my grandmother. "You know that."

He opened the door and stood there a minute before turning back. "I hear the bungalow is going to be for rent come spring."

"You mean back where Dan and I started?" my mother asked.

"Thought I'd mention it, that's all."

"I 'spose you and the children could always move in with us," my grandmother said. She shook her head and followed my grandfather out the door.

Chapter Twenty-Three

GOING TO THE RITZ

My grandparents couldn't fix things. Aunt Belle wouldn't fix things. My father... he was the one who said the word "divorce." I couldn't even fix things with Ruby. Maybe Miss Nickel would know what to do—if I could figure out a way to go see her.

My mother talked a lot about telling the truth. My grandmother even said once that telling a lie would make your nose grow long. I thought maybe she was lying a bit then. So there had to be exceptions, like now, when things were all mixed up and going wrong.

It took my staying awake one whole night to think up a story to tell my mother. The next morning, I waited until I was going out the door to school to say, "Ruby asked me to her house. She's got new paper dolls. She wants me to come this afternoon."

"Are you sure it's all right with her mother?" my mother asked.

"Yeah, it's okay."

She looked up from the pail of Larry's dirty diapers she sorted into the washing machine. Steam rolled from kettles of water boiling on the stove. "You can't stay long. It gets dark early now." She paused. "It's nice you have a friend."

That stopped me for a minute. Did my mother have friends? Maybe you could call people related to us friends. I couldn't think of anyone else ever coming to visit.

At school Ruby didn't talk to me, and I didn't know how to talk to her. Instead I kept thinking about how I would get to Miss Nickel's place. When we had to move from our rooming house, Miss Nickel had to move too. I remembered her saying something about the Ritz Theater on the square. On one of our Saturday afternoons with my father, he had taken Nancy and me to the Ritz to see a western movie. It would be fun to live in a movie house.

After school, I started out at a run along the street we always took to the square. I was going along good when I slipped on some ice and skinned my knee. I limped along for a few steps before running again. My side hurt. The courthouse had to be just up ahead. Finally, above the trees, I could make out the tiniest triangle of the green roof topping the clock tower. I ran again until I had to stop. Panting for breath, I swiped my mitten across my drippy nose and wished I had worn my hood. But I could see the clock. My feet were getting cold so I started to run again. Then I saw the wide green roof Miss Nickel had pointed out from her window in our rooming house.

At last I was on the street edging one side of the courthouse. The orange peaked roof of the Ritz stood at the far corner of the square. Under the roof, three tall, skinny windows cut into yellow stucco looked out from under pink molded arches. Maybe Miss Nickel lived behind one of those windows. Then she could watch the people who moved along the square: fancy dressed women coming out of the *Up Town Ladies Shoppe*, men in overalls coming from the hardware, farm wives in their print dresses coming out of the grocery store, storekeepers in suits coming out of the bank, young girls in flouncy dresses coming from the dime stores. It would be like seeing a movie every day.

An orange tile roof held up by chains stretched over the theater's box office windows and main doors. The box office lady wanted a dime to let me in. She couldn't understand my question about Miss Nickel. I had to wipe my nose again. Maybe the lady thought I was about to cry because she came to the door to let me in.

The lobby was as grand as I remembered—high rounded ceilings, a lighted chandelier even though it was still light outside, thick red carpet, mirrors and different movie posters showing Clark Gable and Judy Garland.

"The matinee is almost over," the lady said.

"I need to see Miss Nickel."

"Miss Nickel?"

"She lives here at the Ritz."

"Honey, nobody lives here. This is a movie theater. Miss Nickel, you say? Oh yes, I think that's the name of the woman who lives in that place behind the theater. I let her sneak into the second show a time or two. She was especially keen to see *Gone with the Wind*."

The lady motioned me to follow her across the lobby where she opened a side door and pointed to an old house with a wooden stairway leading up to a second floor. "See that door at the top of the stairs. Miss Nickel lives up there with some old woman. Her cousin, I think."

She started to close the theater door behind her. "You going to be all right?"

"Miss Nickel will help me," I said.

"You're okay, then? I got to get back to the box office, or I'll be losing my job."

The back of the movie house was ugly dark brick. The house where Miss Nickel lived seemed worse than ours. Along the alley, beer bottles lay on top of dirty clumps of snow. I was afraid there might be rats.

The wooden rail wobbled under my hand as I climbed the stairs. I knocked at the door, but no one came. I knocked again. Still no one. I was turning to go when Miss Nickel opened the door. With stringy brown hair falling around her face, she looked different from the plump, smiley woman I remembered. A heavy sweater over her housedress hung loosely on her.

"Ruth Ann," she said. "Whatever...? Are you by yourself? Come in, come in, child. You're nearly frozen."

She wrapped her arms around me, hugging me to her soft sweater, and I started to blubber. Frankie would call me a crybaby. But I couldn't help it. I blubbered more.

"Come here," she said, leading me to a chair next to a small table. "I've got water on for tea. You won't like tea, but at least it's hot. I'll put extra sugar in it. Take off your coat and mittens." She took a worn quilt from the back of a chair and tucked it around me. "This will warm you up." Huddled inside the quilt, I curled my fingers around the hot mug she gave me and breathed in the steaming tea.

After a couple of swallows, I looked around the room. Darker and smaller than her room in our rooming house, there must not have been space for her cupboard full of pretty dishes. A narrow cot stood against a wall. I wondered what had happened to her pink and yellow and orange "apple-kay" pillows. There was one small window. It showed the theater's brick wall. Snoring sounds and a smell that reminded me of my grandmother's chamber pot came from the partially opened door on the far side of the room.

"Now, Ruth Ann, what is the matter?" Miss Nickel asked.

Words gushed out with my sobs. "My dad is going to divorce us. The undertaker man is going to put my mom in jail, and Ruby's mad at me."

"Slow down, Ruth Ann, slow down here. What do you mean the undertaker man is going to put your mom in jail? That can't be."

"That's what he said, because Mom sold the stupid, old rug she hadn't paid for yet. But Grandpa said he would take care of it."

"Then that's what he will do. If your grandpa said he would take care of it, he will. You don't have to worry about that silly old undertaker man. Okay?"

"You're sure?"

"I'm sure. Now who is Ruby?"

"She was my friend, but I was mean to her."

"How were you mean?"

I almost couldn't say it, the way Ruby was the same as me but not, at least not as others seemed to see it. "I didn't play with her." I thought Miss Nickel might understand the rest just by looking at me.

"Well," she said at last. "You're sorry about that, right?"

"Oh yes."

"You can tell her you're sorry?"

I nodded my head, but I wasn't so sure I could—not with those starched girls watching me. And what if Ruby didn't want to be my friend anymore?

"Now about your folks and a divorce. I'm really sorry to hear that, and I don't have an answer. I've seen both your mom and dad, and there's one thing I do know—your mom loves you and your dad loves you. Neither one is ever going to divorce you."

A voice came from behind the partially opened door. "Em? Who's out there? Em?"

"I'll be there in minute," Miss Nickel called back.

"Em. Emily, I need you." The voice was old and cranky, followed by a tapping sound.

"Bertie, I'll be there."

"Emily." The tapping got louder.

"Someday I'm going to burn that cane," Miss Nickel muttered. "You have to go, Ruth Ann. I'm sorry. Here, I'll help you with your coat and mittens." She took a pink knitted scarf from a peg beside the outside door. "Maybe this will help." She tied it around my head and wound it around my neck.

"Em—il—y!"

"You must hurry now, Ruth Ann, to get home before dark." Miss Nickel opened the door leading to the wooden stairs. Stepping out onto the landing, she gave me a quick hug. "Bless you, child." And she was gone.

Chapter Twenty-Four

THE BLUE CROCK

My mother didn't even notice my scarf when I came in the door. She just said, "Thank God, you're home. Did you see Frankie anywhere?" I shook my head, and she turned back to the window.

That night and nights following, I tucked the pink scarf under my pillow to remind myself that everything was going to be all right. Like Miss Nickel said, my grandfather would pay the undertaker man so my mother wouldn't have to go to jail. But come morning, I'd still wake up shivering, thinking maybe the policeman would knock on our door.

Every day I wondered if my mother would be there when I got home from school. I'd rush to our house, pulling Nancy along with me. But before turning the last corner, I would hang back. Maybe my mother and Larry wouldn't be there. Maybe there'd be a policeman parked in the driveway.

After seeing my mother in the kitchen where she was supposed to be, I hung my coat on my peg behind the door and sat at my place at the table for my half-cup of milk. Fixing us bread spread with my grandmother's apple butter, she asked the usual, "How was school?"

Her eyes went someplace else while Nancy blabbed about some boy in her class marking up her spelling paper, pulling her hair after Nancy tattled to the teacher. I wanted to tell my mother about the Civil War game the kids played at recess, dividing up sides of North and South. They said Ruby had to be on the South side. No one else went over to the South side. Not even me.

Was that what divorce was like? Everyone on different sides? My mother was already off on her side. She had been that way ever since the rug thing. Didn't she know my grandfather was going to take care of that? Sometimes I would hear her crying in her room. Other times, she'd put on her coat and go into the closed-off living room to play the piano. She didn't play hum-along songs. She beat out sounds that went on and on, filling up the kitchen and pounding against our ears.

And Frankie was no better about getting home on time. It was like he didn't want to get stuck staying with us kids. Or maybe he was trying to make up with Sam and Buck at the pool hall. I knew better than to tell my mother about what I'd seen there.

One night Frankie was really late. She kept going back and forth to the window, jerking the curtain back to peer out, but the streetlight showed only the empty sidewalk. Slowly she'd push the curtain back in place. She poured herself a cup of coffee and sat stirring it at the table. When I went to bed, she was still sitting there, stirring her coffee. The next morning the curtain drooped away from the window. She sat at the table, her fingers tracing the rim of the black-ringed cup.

That morning a policeman did come to our door. He had Frankie with him. Over our cereal bowls, Nancy and I gaped at our brother as the policeman steered him into the kitchen. My mother was out of her chair and standing in the center of the room. I remembered Uncle Josh's story about Lot's wife being turned into a pillar of salt. That's what my mother looked like.

"I'm sorry, ma'am," said the policeman, closing the door behind him. "I found this boy down in the gutter by the pool hall. He says he's yours."

My mother nodded, stock still. This boy didn't look like our Frankie—the big curly-headed brother that high-school girls giggled over. This was a scruffy-haired stray someone had left out in a storm.

"Thought he might as well sleep it off at home rather than in the jailhouse." The policeman let go of Frankie, but his voice went sharper. "Next time, it'll be different."

No longer Lot's wife, she stepped forward and took Frankie's other arm, pulling him away from the policeman. "Sir, there'll be no next time."

I knew that "no talking back" tone. The policeman must have known it too. "Yes, ma'am. I'll hold you to that, ma'am."

My mother opened the kitchen door. "Thank you, officer." She didn't sound the least bit thankful.

As soon as the screen door shut behind the man, she let Frankie have it. "You're bringing the police to our door? How could you?"

He didn't answer.

"What you been doing, Frankie?"

"Nothing."

"From the smell of you, it's not nothing."

There was a stink about him. It made me think of the pool hall. Now my mother would find out about Sam and Buck and the beer drinking. Nancy up and asked, "You puke or something, Frankie?"

He didn't even bother to give her a dirty look. Under the weight of his stained coat, he couldn't seem to stand up straight.

"What's got into you, Frankie?" my mother asked. "It's those kids you been hanging out with. I knew they were no good."

"It's not them," Frankie mumbled.

"I'm going to call your dad about this."

Frankie's head jerked up. "Good one, Mom. Good one," he said in a voice that would have got me swatted. "You gonna call him at that woman's house?"

It was like Frankie had knocked the breath out of her, the way she stepped back. Remembering us, she said, "Get your coats on, girls, and go on to school."

I needed to get my scarf first. As I wound it around my neck, my mother sent Frankie upstairs, telling him to get cleaned up and get some sleep. She called after him, "We're not through with this, young man."

At school that day, I looked at the other kids' faces, wondering if they knew about the policeman coming to our house. I rolled up my scarf and pushed it to the back of my desk where I could touch it. Maybe my mother had already gone to the corner grocery to call my father. Maybe he would come and fix things. During singing time, Ruby didn't sing along with us on the song *Old Black Joe*, though she usually sang louder than everyone. I didn't feel like singing either.

At recess, I wore my scarf, but I couldn't talk to the starched girls, laughing about something near the swings. I couldn't even tell Ruby about the policeman. Probably she was still mad at me because of the time I fibbed to her. I had told Miss Nickel I'd tell Ruby I was sorry, but I still didn't know how. Now, Ruby stood alone by the schoolhouse wall, like she had that other time.

The girls at the swings were huddled together. I went up to Ruby. "See my new scarf. My friend that lives by the Ritz Theater gave it to me." Ruby didn't say anything. I lifted a pink tail to her. "Feel, it's soft.

Ruby reached out to touch the pink wool. "Yeah, it's real pretty."

"Yeah." I leaned against the wall beside her.

That afternoon there was someone parked in our driveway. It wasn't a police car. It was my father's truck. He had come. Nancy took off running. I tried to think what it could mean as I crossed the mud-crusted yard into the grimy porch where I saw my father's overshoes, one standing upright, the other fallen on its side. Nancy had left the door halfway open. I closed it behind me, trying to make no noise.

My mother was over by the window in her rocker, holding Larry. She was not rocking. Still wearing his roughened suede jacket, my father stood next to the table where Frankie sat, hunched over, his hair mussed up like he'd just got out of bed. I got the feeling they'd been talking for a while, and my father knew about the policeman and the beer. Frankie was really in trouble now.

No one was happy to see Nancy or me. Everyone went quiet as we hung up our coats. I hung my scarf next to my father's hat. Finally my mother said, "There's bread, Ruth Ann." I moved to the cupboard, cut off two slices from her daily baked loaf, and we carried the bread to the old quilt spread near the heat register where the rug used to be.

Now sitting next to Frankie at the table, my father wiped his hand over his combed-back hair. "Where'd you get the stuff, Frankie?"

"I told you," said my mother. "It's those kids…"

"Frankie?" my father asked again.

"At the pool hall."

"What you doing, hanging out there?"

"I got friends there."

"Some friends!"

"What about your friend?" Frankie made *friend* sound like a dirty word.

My father's eyes shot to my mother. She turned her face to the window. "I don't know what you think you know," he said to Frankie, "but we're talking about you here. Worrying your mother. A policeman bringing you home."

Frankie lifted his head. His eyes were red, but there was something sharp about the look he gave my father. Frankie stood up like he didn't want to hear anymore. My father rose to stand in front of him. I was surprised that Frankie was almost as tall as him. I thought my father was surprised too.

"Listen, Frank...." He reached out to Frankie but changed his mind and moved to the door. "Frank." He turned back again. "I don't have nothing to say for myself. Except sometimes... sometimes a man don't use good sense." He took his hat from the rack. "But that's no call for you to be messing up your life."

"You say," said Frankie and headed for the stairs.

"Yes, I say. I got my eye on you now, son." My father put his hat squarely on his head. "There'll be no policeman bringing you home again."

My father left. He didn't even talk to me or Nancy.

When we came home from school the next day, Frankie was already there, sitting in the rocker, picking at his guitar. The notes didn't sound like music. He shoved the guitar aside. "This is for the birds. Why can't I go see Buck and Sam?"

My mother answered, "You know why."

Nancy went to Frankie and started to pick up his guitar.

"Leave it alone," he barked at her. "Mom, what am I supposed to do cooped up here with little kids?"

"You could go down and scoop some coal into the furnace for one thing."

Nancy reached for the guitar again.

"I said to leave it alone."

"Frankie, there's no use growling at your sister. And there's plenty of work to do around here."

About that time, my father's truck wheeled onto the gravel driveway. I opened the kitchen door for him. He stood there like he wasn't sure whether he should come in.

"Frank, you want to go along with me? I had to pull Jim Scott's Farmall into the garage here. He wants me to do some work on it. You could help me."

"I don't wanna help you."

I couldn't believe my ears. "I'll help you, Daddy."

He walked past me. "How about it, Frank?"

"I don't want to."

My mother didn't say anything.

"It's like the tractor we worked on last summer," my father went on. "You were the one that got it running."

"I gotta scoop coal for Mom," Frankie said.

She sighed. "I can do that like I do every day. Go on, Frankie. You were just complaining about nothing to do."

Frankie put on his coat and followed my father out the door. Neither one said anything. Frankie climbed into the truck. He stayed close to the door and looked out the window. The next afternoon my father was there again to take Frankie to the garage. Frankie grumbled a little, but he went. When they came back to the house, they sat in the truck talking. The motor ran for a long time.

Saturday was supposed to be the day for Nancy and me to go with my father. Instead, he just brought us a sack of candy. Like the Saturday nights when we used to go into Littleton, we had to count out the pieces, six for Nancy and six for me. Frankie got to go with my father. They were gone all day.

During the next week, we got so we expected my father to come by to pick up Frankie and go off to the garage. My father usually stayed a little while asking Nancy and me about schoolwork or playing with Larry. Sometimes, I'd see him watching my mother while she fixed our snacks or started supper. Her eyes would go to him too, then drop like she didn't want him to catch her looking. One night I forgot to tuck my scarf under my pillow.

The next Saturday Frankie was off with my father again. Doing some hauling, my mother said. When they returned, my father brought in a bag of groceries and handed them to her.

I couldn't get in a word edgewise. Frankie talked a mile a minute—something about buying a couple of old Chevys. "You wait. I'll turn them into one whiz-bang of a car."

"Money on junk cars?" My mother held a white-wrapped package of meat.

"The garage man wants rid of them, but he'll give us some time to work on them there." My father lowered his voice. "It's a sure sight better than the pool hall."

On the days following, Frankie beat us home from school so he'd be there when my father came to pick him up to go to the garage. One night my mother said he might as well stay for supper. "That is, if there's no other place you want to be?"

My father looked at her. "There's no other place I want to be."

As I cleared the table, my mother asked, "Danny, is Frankie all right?"

"He's okay. He works good when he wants. You know, he's got your pa's hands—those big hands, strong enough to build anything."

"Like our bungalow."

"Well, I got some blisters on that too," he said.

"It was a good house."

"Yeah." He paused. "I hear it's for rent again."

"I heard that too."

On evenings following, he stayed more often for supper. He and Frankie would come in from the garage, wash their greasy hands in the bathroom sink, and my mother wouldn't even yell at them for leaving Lava soap smears all over the towels.

My father's being there didn't do much good for Nancy or me, since Frankie took up his time talking about valves, carburetors, spark plugs, and other boring stuff. Frankie went on and on about the car he'd have some day.

I was getting sick of this car talk. "Who'd want a junk car?"

He snapped a tea towel at me. "You just wait, Smarty Pants. After I get that car shined up, those spoke wheels painted a spanking yellow, you'll beg for a ride."

"Slow down here, Frankie," my mother said. "Remember there's a little thing like having a license."

Sometimes long after us kids had gone to bed, my parents talked. When their voices turned soft and easy or one of them would laugh, I went to sleep. Then came the morning when we ran down for breakfast, and my father was still there. Frankie was the last to come downstairs. My mother brought a blue crock of milk to the table and stood watching Frankie, like maybe he wasn't going to sit down. After he slid into his chair, she took her place at the table. My father nodded to us to bow our heads, and he said the blessing like he always had on the farm. From the blue crock, she poured milk into cups and passed one to each of us.

My father looked up at us, grinning. "You kids better start packing. We're moving again—this time together—back to the bungalow where all of you, except for Larry here, were born."

Nancy and I were on our feet, jumping up and down, hugging him, asking, "When? How soon?" We danced around the table, laughing. Larry started laughing too and clapped his hands. That made Frankie laugh. My mother had left the table and moved to the window. She stood there, her lips apart, not laughing, not smiling.

PART THREE
THE BUNGALOW

Chapter Twenty-Five

MARCH

We were moving again, this time together. After all those months of my parents being mad at each other and living in separate places, three of us kids were squished between them in my father's truck, bumping over dirt roads. With Frankie riding in the back atop mismatched furniture and mattresses, we probably looked like something out of *The Grapes of Wrath,* but there was no California for us, just the Iowa bungalow where it started.

Faded photos in our family album showed the bungalow being built on the farm my grandparents had bought for my parents. There it was, walls and trusses open to the sky. Uncle Stu, my grandfather and father up in the rafters, nailing them in place. That was back before Frankie or I was born, back before this Depression thing everyone was talking about now.

My memories of living in the house were as dim as those old photos. But the Bungalow was not something that could be forgotten. The only road between our house and my grandmother's place led us right past it. Like a sore not to be touched, it was always there.

Whenever my mother told stories about their early years in the bungalow, it sounded like a happy, shining place. There was no shine to it that cloudy day in March. I wondered how my mother felt as she walked from the truck, down the rutted lane, past the well with its rusted pump to the cracked cement next to the back stoop. A chunk of cement wobbled under her feet as she stepped up on the broken boards of the back stoop. She pulled at the screen door, then jerked back as the torn screen bit into her hand. Again, she grasped the screen's tiny knob, made from an empty spool of thread—probably something the last farmwife had nailed there—before pushing open the wood door.

The smell of long unused rooms closed down on me as I followed her into the kitchen.

"Mice," my mother said. I had almost forgotten that part of farm life: the trails of mouse droppings leading to their nests of lint, bits of grass or twigs found in corners.

She took off the headscarf covering her dark hair, and she stood there wadding the material in her large hands, seemingly stuck in the weak light from the window.

I wondered why my grandparents weren't there to meet us. Their farmhouse was just a half-mile away, but there was no sign they had been in the house. No simmering pots steamed atop the wood stove. It waited, cold.

Leaving Nancy and Larry in the truck cab with Frankie, my father came to the door. He hesitated. I wondered if he was afraid my mother might suddenly declare she would have no part of this. She was going back to town. He stepped forward. "I'll get a fire started. I brought some coal, and there's surely some wood in the barn or one of the sheds."

"Tell Frankie to bring the broom," she said. "And to pump me some water."

With the broom she brushed down cobwebs from the black stovepipe where it curved to the chimney. After my father had loaded the range with coal plus bits of wood and corncobs, she used the broom on the top of the range too, before scrubbing it with rags and water.

My father was going out for more wood to fire up the living room stove when we heard the Nash. My grandfather stopped at the end of the lane, took something from the back seat, and walked to us carrying a large pot. My grandmother stayed in the car.

My grandfather approached my father, my grandfather in his Oshkosh coat and overalls, my father in his suede jacket. Shiny with wear, it was open over his tan shirt. I hadn't noticed before: my grandfather was bigger and taller than my father. Square shouldered, my father gave no sign of noticing it either.

"Morning, Mr. Hinrichson," he said.

"Morning, Dan." Stepping up on the stoop, my grandfather moved a heavy shoe against the broken board. "I'll bring over something to fix that."

Without saying anything more, he came into the house and placed the pot on the range. "Beef and noodles."

"Mama's not coming in?" my mother asked.

"You know your mama."

"I thought she'd be glad."

"Oh, she is. She'll come around. It'll take some getting used to—having Dan back here."

"Guess she'll never forget that day Dan couldn't make the mortgage payment," my mother said. "We're not likely to, either."

"Your mama said she'd keep the young'uns if that'd help. So you can get things in order."

He looked around the barren room and the pantry that led off it. He moved to the living room. His body nearly filled the doorway, but I squeezed past him. The room was divided by floor cabinets topped by wood posts that rose to the ceiling. On the far wall near the chimney for the heating stove, wallpaper hung loose, curling down.

"Sort of socks you in the stomach, don't it?" he said. "The way renters let everything run down. Remember when it was all new? Remember the smell of new lumber?" He crossed the wood floor to the cabinets. One of the glass panes was broken, but he ran a large hand over a wood panel. "Remember the hours of sanding and varnishing? How they shone?"

My mother nodded. "They were beautiful." There were tears in her dark eyes. "All of it was beautiful."

He straightened up and went back to the kitchen. "I hope this will be a new beginning for you, girl."

"I hope so too, Daddy."

On Monday following the move, my father saw us across the railroad tracks. Then Nancy and I were on our own to walk the dirt road, past the cornfield that once belonged to my grandfather, past his house, to the country school. The one-room schoolhouse was much like the one we had left that October day before that stuff in Centerville happened, back when my parents were mad at each other.

This schoolroom had the same blackboard across the front, the same smells of chalk dust, sweeping compounds, firewood, and kids days away from their Saturday night baths. A boy named Jerry made me think of that other Jerry of the threshing accident, but I couldn't imagine wandering pastures and threshing fields with this Jerry with his dirty fingernails and droopy overalls.

Nancy sat near the teacher in one of the small desks. I was mid-way back sharing a mid-sized desk with a girl about my age. She didn't seem to mind my moving in on her. No one seemed to mind our moving in on them. In spite of the once-over the kids gave us, I realized they knew about Nancy and me. Knew our parents, our grandparents. My mother had gone to this school with the Jensen girls—now known as the old maid Jensen sisters who lived in a weathered house up the hill from my grandmother's. One of those old maid sisters stood before us as our teacher.

There were no Black children here. This was a place where you couldn't even mention them. Certainly not one who had been your friend.

The best thing about this school was that it was so close to my grandparents' house. One of them waved at us every morning when we walked by, and my grandmother would run after us with caps or scarves if she thought we weren't dressed warmly enough. "What's your mother thinking of?" she'd mutter. After school we could stop at their place for hot cocoa and just-churned butter melting on bread right out of the oven.

But it wasn't all hot cocoa and hugs, it was checking spelling and arithmetic papers. It was also little comments about my father. "What's he doing running into Centerville all the time?" And she never stepped inside our bungalow. "No matter how hard your mom scrubs, she'll never get the renter smell out of that house." Then she'd be back on my father again. "His gallivanting days better be over."

Gallivanting sounded like a fun thing to me, but the way she said it, maybe it wasn't.

Other times she'd say, "Don't Dan know there's field work to be done?"

I wanted to say he did too work in the fields. When we went to school, I'd see him out there, reins tied at the small of his back, as he followed my grandfather's team of horses. After school, my father would still be out there walking back and forth or riding on the seat of his plow, carving out straight rows of glistening black earth. When he came home at night, he'd sit down on our back stoop, take off his boots, and pour dirt out of them.

I wanted to tell her all that, but I didn't. I took another bite of her fresh bread. It didn't taste so good.

The first week or two, we'd come home from my grandmother's house to find my mother tired out from washing down walls and scrubbing floors. At the supper table one night, she said, "It'll never be like it was." When my father turned away, I wasn't sure she was talking about the house.

Spring was late in coming. Cleaning up mud tracked in from the lane and barnyard, plus having to keep fires going in the kitchen and living room, didn't help my mother's mood any. Maybe she thought of my grandmother's house where steam hissing and gurgling through radiators kept the whole house warm. And hearing my grandmother talk about getting her baby chicks started didn't help either. "She has a brooder house to keep her chicks in," my mother muttered, "not a drafty, falling down hen house."

After a few days she must have decided that was no excuse for not doing what needed to be done. She ordered eggs ready to be hatched from the hatchery.

I didn't know that meant chickens in the house until Nancy and I came home from school to find a large wooden box set up on legs and standing in the living room where the dining table should have been.

My mother called the box an incubator. Wire netting stretched from edge to edge of the box. Resting on a cushion of straw were eggs ready to hatch.

Nancy and I stood on tiptoe to watch baby chicks peck their way out of their shells. A drowned-looking yellow head emerged first. Its eyes wide and wild, the chick pecked at the rest of the shell. At last it struggled free, rested on scaly bent legs, and righted itself, flapping feeble, matted wings against its still wet body.

It's ugly, I thought, and turned to the other chicks, a day or two old. They were fluttery, golden puffs. When my mother let us, Nancy and I liked to cup a soft chick in our hands. I didn't mind the tiny digging claws, but I definitely didn't like the chick pooping in my hands.

"Chickens getting born smell bad," Nancy said.

"I know," my mother said, "but we have to keep them inside where it's warm."

Every day the cheep, cheep of the chicks got louder, and every day the stink got worse.

The grass in our front yard greened up. I saw a robin. Frankie and I raked away the broken branches and shriveled fruit as the pear tree blossomed anew. The incubator and chickens were moved to the hen house. My mother was scrubbing walls again and making curtains for the living room.

The bungalow became our home. There was a clean smell to the rooms, rag rugs on polished floors. My mother let me decide how I wanted to arrange furniture in the bedroom for Nancy and me. From a box not opened the whole time we lived in the Washburn Street house and the house near the levee, she let me unpack the family pictures and arrange them atop our piano. My parents' wedding picture was at the bottom of the box. She didn't say anything when I put it on the piano.

The school term ended early so that the bigger boys could help their fathers on the farm. Even Frankie's high school in town ended early. So when he wasn't in the fields, I had him to put up with, poking me in the ribs or swiping from my plate that piece of meat I saved for last. Fortunately, he wasn't around much because it was planting time. He was usually working with my father or grandfather.

My mother itched for planting time too. She walked across a patch of ground next to the house. It was a mess of tangled weeds. "Guess renters weren't interested in gardening." She tugged at a stubborn stalk. "We had our first garden here. Dan helped me with the planting, and in the evenings we worked at the weeding. We had ourselves a good garden."

Maybe my father thought about a good garden too, because a couple of days later he forked up the weeds leaving behind clumps of glistening black soil. In the evenings he, my mother, and Frankie worked with spades, rakes, and hoes breaking up clods.

One night after supper, I was helping my mother plant rock-like peas in the rows she had hoed out when Nancy begged to go barefoot. My mother said it was too early, but Nancy kept begging and she gave in. Nancy and Larry yanked their shoes and socks off. Of course, I had to too. The ground was colder against my bare feet than I expected.

Nancy and Larry ran back and forth, laughing at their coated toes and footprints left in the soft, pebbly soil. My parents looked at each other, and they laughed too. I thought Nancy was acting silly and went back to helping my mother, pressing beans now in a different row. With the hoe swinging big and awkward in my hands, I tried to smooth dirt over the beans like my father showed me.

Before I knew it, we had finished the planting. Evening cooled and birds twittered as they nestled in trees. On the hill behind the house, the barn was like a paper cutout pasted on a reddish-orange sky.

Larry and Nancy ran on to have my father wash their feet at the pump. My mother looked over the newly worked earth, string stretched beside straight rows of tamped down soil.

"We're going to have ourselves a good garden," I said.

She smiled. "Yes, Ruth Ann, we are."

Chapter Twenty-Six

GRANDMOTHER'S HOUSE

Before everything changed again, summer meant lazy walks between our house and my grandmother's house, counting hollyhocks standing like ladies in waiting along the lane to the barn, climbing trees in the orchard, treading through tall pasture grass to the mail box with my grandmother to get her weekly letter from Aunt Belle.

The inside of my grandmother's house offered all kinds of places to play hide and seek—behind the giant mothball-scented blanket chest full of my grandmother's quilts or under the brass bed where Uncle Lars and Aunt Belle slept when they visited. The parlor where the piano stood in company with potted ferns and a doily-armored sofa was a forbidden room. So of course that's where we headed whenever my grandmother was busy on the back porch or in her garden.

Nancy would not go into the parlor alone, not even to hammer away on the piano. She was afraid of the tight-lipped ancestors whose piercing eyes stared down on her from the portraits on the walls.

That's the way my grandmother expected family pictures to be. She had a thing about smiling for pictures. "If that person dies," she'd say. "You'd have to look at his smiling face. And who wants to look at a smiling dead person?"

Strangely, my grandmother didn't seem to mind looking at pictures of dead people. In the front room where my grandfather listened to the radio or read the newspaper while my grandmother did her mending or studied her Bible, a picture of her mother in her casket was prominently displayed behind the curved glass door of the china cabinet.

It was kept locked at all times. My grandmother showed me the key, saying, "If the house ever catches on fire, get that picture out."

In our running room to room, Nancy and I gave a wide berth to that cabinet with its glass door. Mostly we were careful not to let my grandmother catch us running in the house because her face and dark eyes could almost double for one of those stern portraits if she caught us doing something we weren't supposed to.

She was willing to put up with our running the length of the porch that wound around the front of the house. Back and forth we ran until we sank down on my grandfather's swing, panting for breath. From there we could watch my grandmother work. Wearing a sunbonnet and apron to cover her print housedress, she'd be down on her knees planting her flower garden. It wasn't something she wanted help with. She knew how she wanted those purple petunias, moss roses, and marigolds to fan out, creating what she called a flowery apron for her house.

June sputtered into July, sizzling hot. A walk to her house became too much effort. Worse yet, we couldn't walk it barefoot, because the beaten-down track burnt our feet. So Nancy and I lazed around our house, talking about Aunt Belle and Uncle Lars coming on the Fourth of July. It was a get-together that my grandmother had at her house every year. Uncle Stu and Aunt Violet would come too.

I wondered if my father would be going. He hadn't been invited to my grandmother's house since we moved back. But I had other things to think about, like homemade ice cream and how my grandfather would get ice from Littleton to his house without its melting.

Excited about the firecrackers Uncle Lars would buy for us after he arrived, Frankie scouted out the area across the Missouri line every day to see if tents for selling fireworks had been set up yet.

My mother and grandmother kept to the work of getting ready. Pausing only to mop sweat from their faces with their aprons, they killed and dressed chickens, fired up the range to bake bread, pies, and cakes, dug potatoes, shelled peas, and set the big dining room table with my grandmother's best dishes.

Heat clung to us like a damp shirt, dragging down our shoulders and arms. The evening before the big dinner, my parents looked to the fiery sunset and said maybe there'd be rain to cool things off a bit.

I was too excited to sleep much. The train rumbled past, and when the sound of the whistle drifted off, so did I. There was another rumbling, this time of thunder. Rain beat the roof and slashed the windows. My mother got up to disconnect the phone and close the panes. My grandmother, a real scaredy-cat when it came to storms, was probably doing the same at her house.

Thunder and lightning were getting something fierce now. A bright flash made me pull my pillow over my head, but I wasn't quick enough to shut out the shotgun crack of thunder. Nancy jumped up and went running to my parents' room. I stayed under my pillow, pressing it against my ears. When the thunder quieted, I could sleep again.

I woke up to someone pounding on our kitchen door. My father was talking, a cry from my mother.

I swung out of bed and ran to the kitchen. Frankie was there too. All of us were in our night clothes, listening to the man and woman in the doorway. Old hats dripping over wet hair and clothes, the man and woman's words bumped into each other. "It's burning fast. You gotta come." "We're up high—that's the way we seen it. Something like a dark cloud at first. Then flames leaping up." "I told you something got hit." "By the time we got dressed and got down there..." "Bring buckets." "Buckets won't help much now." "Roads turned down right muddy." "My old car made it through just fine." "Poor Miz Hinrichson. She's beside herself—trying to get things out." "Dr. Lars, he's trying to keep them back, saying they'll get burned alive."

The woman turned to my mother. "You know your mama, Sarah. She ain't easy to stop. You gotta go. I'll stay here with the young'uns. Don't you worry none about them."

My parents and Frankie rushed back to their rooms to get dressed. My mother had trouble finding her shoes.

"I'm coming too." I turned to my room.

"No, Ruth Ann," she said, pulling on her dress. "You stay here and help Mrs. Long take care of Nancy and Larry."

"You might take along an extra dress and maybe a coat for your mother," said the woman. "Don't know that they got any clothes out."

I recognized the woman now. She and her husband lived up the hill next to the Jensen sisters.

Running around like a chicken with its head cut off, my mother grabbed up things to take with her. Then they were gone. Mrs. Long was nice enough, but I didn't have anything to say to her. My grandmother's house was burning down, and I was stuck at home, waiting for it to get light.

After a while Mrs. Long snored in my mother's rocker. I stretched out on the floor and maybe I slept some before I smelled smoke. I went outside. Over the fields running to my grandmother's house, the sun was coming up. The cloud hanging in the sky was smoke.

I ran back into the house, pulled on my dress, and stepped into my shoes. Mrs. Long stirred in the rocker. "I'm going to Grandma's." I headed for the door.

"Ruth Ann," she said, barely awake.

"I walk it all the time. I'll be fine." And I was off, running down the lane. She called after me, but I kept going.

The road to my grandmother's was no longer baked clay. It was slippery, slidey mud. I should have left off my shoes. The closer I got, the sharper the smell of smoke. I passed the hedge trees along my grandfather's oat field, passed the orchard. The smoke was real now, stinging my eyes, clogging my nose, coating my tongue. Cars were parked along the ornamental fence and gate, marking the front yard. The sidewalk from the gate led to more smoke, spinning over charred masses of rubble.

Beyond the haze, just yards from where the house should have been, stood the smoke house. The gray wood of the building was a scorched brown, but for some reason it was still standing.

People—neighbors, I guessed—clumped together, talking or staring. A woman broke away to me. "Ruth Ann, what are you doing here?" It was Miss Jensen, my teacher.

"Where's the house?" I asked.

"It's gone, I'm afraid. Let's find your mother." She led me around other clumps of people, around scattered pieces of furniture, small tables, some family pictures, a blue clock, and a tall cabinet standing on uneven ground.

My mother was over by the big maple tree with Aunt Belle and some women I didn't know. They hovered around my grandmother who was wrapped in a quilt and sitting on a kitchen chair. Her face was the only one not streaked by tears. She wanted to know if Uncle Stu and Aunt Violet had arrived.

I got a scolding from my mother and lots of questions about Nancy, Larry, and Mrs. Long.

"I wanted to see," I told her.

"Well, you're here. Don't get too close."

There wasn't much danger of that. The blackened foundation was surrounded by hot coals spitting against wet grass. Like stacks of blocks left untended by a child, only chimneys stood where the kitchen and front room had been. I moved among groups of people, taking in their talk.

"When we got here," one man said, "Dan and Mr. Hinrichson were up on the roof with buckets of water trying to put the fire out, but everyone kept yelling at them to get down."

The woman hanging onto him said, "You should've heard the weird noises those gas lights were making—like they were going to explode or something. I wasn't going to let my Elmer go into that house."

I followed neighbors as they pointed at ash-covered forms. Yes, that was the kitchen range—and that thick charred slab—that must have been the sideboard for her good dishes. They oh-ed and ah-ed over an unbroken plate on top of a pile of ashes. In the ashy pit that was once the cellar, I spotted what looked like ribs of dead animals. They were radiators, broken free from their steam pipes. Down in that mess was a small twisted mass of wires. It was the bird cage, I knew, for Mickey, my grandmother's canary.

Others pointed to charred studs hanging over what was left of the piano. "Got stuck in the doorway," said Uncle Lars. "That's as far as we could get it."

He waved a bandaged hand at a discolored heap lying in a far corner of the foundation. "I must have been holding onto the brass bedstead when the lightning struck. Burned me good. To top that, I ran outside without my shoes and got my feet shocked on wet grass."

"They didn't save much," said a woman watching Frankie and my father as they picked up the few rescued things to carry into the shelter of the smoke house. "You better take this piece," said another, pointing to the tall cabinet. "I don't know why, but I guess Miz Hinrichson was determined to get it out of the house. They say she kept muttering about a key. Then she pulled the whole thing out. A rug got balled up between the legs, but she got it out."

I could have told them why. It was my grandmother's china cabinet. The casket picture of my great-grandmother was still behind the locked glass door.

Chapter Twenty-Seven

A GOOD PLENTY

Aunt Violet was sobbing. Immediately after she and Uncle Stu had finally arrived, she broke though the circle of women surrounding my grandmother, threw her arms around her, and sobbed. In the shadow of the maple tree, Uncle Stu remained, his mouth tightened like he wanted to cry too. But, of course, men didn't cry. Frankie knew that. And if girls like me wanted to play with boys, they didn't cry either.

Her face pressed into my grandmother's shoulder, Aunt Violet sobbed. Her tears must have soaked my grandmother's dress. She soon had enough of that. "For heaven's sake, Violet, get ahold of yourself. It's not your house."

"It was home," cried Aunt Violet and sobbed louder.

Some woman I had never seen before started to cry. "Go on, Violet," said my grandmother. "You're getting everyone all stirred up."

My mother and Aunt Belle led Aunt Violet away. There were tears in their eyes too. My grandmother watched as they walked away from the charred ruins to the orchard. I was surprised it was as green as it had been the day before.

My grandmother stood up, wearing my mother's dress over her nightgown. The dress was too short for her. She turned to her son. "Stuart, what do we do now?"

~ ~ ~

In the days following, Aunt Violet could not go near what had been her home without sobbing. Maybe that's the reason she got the job of looking after us kids. She didn't let dishes in the sink or our unmade beds get in the way of playing a quick game of tag or being down on the floor with us, her plump body bent over building blocks and coloring books. Nor did she mind my taking off to see what was going on at my grandmother's place.

The night after the fire, my grandparents surprised us with their decision to go home with Uncle Stu and Aunt Violet—if she could stop crying long enough. My grandmother had turned down my mother's invitation saying she didn't want to crowd in on her and us children. Aunt Belle and Uncle Lars had already returned home because he had patients to see. Besides they lived too far away. That left Uncle Stu's house. After a couple of nights of staying with Aunt Violet, my grandmother announced that she and my grandfather would be moving into the smoke house.

"You can't do that," my mother said.

"Of course, we can," said my grandmother. "We need to be here to keep after things."

Later that day, my mother and father stood near the edge of the broken foundation, looking over the ruin. Her eyes went to a fruit jar someone had found in the ash-heaped cellar, buried there among twisted metal jar lids and shards of exploded crockery and glass. Something about the fruit jar—unbroken, not even cracked, the apples still inside it, now well cooked—must have set her off. Suddenly she was crying, and my father wrapped his arms around her. They held onto each other that way for what seemed a long time. My grandmother watched from the smoke house doorway. Then she turned and went inside.

The next morning Aunt Violet was at the bungalow to stay with Nancy and Larry while my mother was back at my grandmother's place working to make the smoke house livable. It would take some doing, I thought as I tagged along after her. No bigger than the parlor had been, the smoke house was what she called a "Ben-of-all-trades," crammed with wash tubs, boilers, milk buckets, garden tools, my grandfather's tools, fruit jars, kettles for canning, and harnesses in need of mending.

In the midst of this clutter, a full-sized bed had been hauled down from Aunt Violet's spare room.

It seemed to me that making the place livable was a little like playing house—like Nancy and I did when we pushed back scoops, pitchforks, and milk buckets in the barn and turned the milk stool into a chair and the work bench into a table.

Frankie moved what he could from the smoke house to the barn and sheds while my mother and grandmother brushed down walls and scrubbed away some of the mixed odors of hickory smoke, soured milk, lye soap, firewood, and kerosene.

They worked against the jarring sounds of sledge hammers knocking down the foundation, and against the roar of my father's Case tractor as he pulled heat radiators from the rubble. We watched holding our breath as my grandfather and Uncle Stu bound chains and ropes around the hot water furnace so that the tractor could pull it from where it had fallen into the cellar.

Uncle Stu spotted a crack in one of the furnace pipes and said the whole thing might as well be hauled to the ditch.

"It was new," my grandfather said. "I'll fix it."

Word had gone out over the party line that my grandparents were fixing to stay in the smoke house. Some people thought it was pretty funny that the uppity Hinrichsons were down to living in a smoke house. Someone had actually said, "Served them right after that bankruptcy thing they pulled some years back." That got repeated until my grandmother heard it. But when those neighbors stopped by, bringing food, bedding, lanterns, pots and pans, they saw my grandmother standing tall and proud on the top step leading into the smoke house. Forced to look up at her, they were quick to say, "Yes, staying in the smoke house was a smart thing, a brave thing to do."

The woman who brought a flowered tablecloth and lace curtains for the smokehouse's one window became my grandmother's friend for life.

Day after day the clearing went on. My father and Frankie were usually at my grandparents' place helping, but they came back to our house for meals. On top of farm chores, gardening and canning, my grandfather was going to the lumber yard, pricing and figuring. My grandmother was drawing and redrawing plans, complaining about how much smaller the new house would have to be.

My grandfather said, "It'll be good and plenty."

He and my father mixed sand, cement, and water for the new foundation, and finally it was poured in place.

The Sunday after they had hauled the new lumber from the train station to my grandfather's farm, my mother said we were going to church. I was a little surprised. We hadn't gone to church since we moved back. She said neighbors kept after her. She guessed it was time.

Right on the Missouri line, the church was a small frame building, not much bigger than our country school house. My parents had gone there as kids. Maybe I did too, when I was real little, but I didn't remember it.

We were late in arriving, so we had to go to the front for a seat, our shoes clattering against the wood floor. Everyone looked at us. And they kept looking at us. I knew several of the people there—the couple who lived on the next farm, kids from our new school, my teacher, and my grandparents.

People didn't pay much attention to the piano playing, but they sang loud. The preacher was loud too. Swinging his arms and punching the air, he repeated the word *sin*. I didn't think he was talking about me.

After the service, the minister cornered my parents, asking if they'd be coming back to help with the singing and piano playing. My mother mumbled something and hurried after my grandparents to ask them to come to our house for Sunday dinner.

My grandfather up and answered, "That sounds mighty good, Pet. We'll be there."

Now I knew why my mother had spent extra time cleaning the day before, why we had to pick up our rooms and make our beds, why she had got up early to kill and dress two chickens.

We hurried on home. My grandparents must have done a lot of visiting after church because by the time they arrived at our house, the chicken was frying and potatoes and vegetables were set to boil.

My grandmother took a long look around when she came in: the rag rugs, the flouncy curtains at the windows, the old, but starched and ironed tablecloth, the song books on the music rack, and the family pictures atop the piano.

"Brings back a lot of memories." Her voice was softer than usual. "Nice memories."

She smiled. It was a gentle smile, maybe a sad smile. I reached out and took her hand, wanting to tell her that even though her home was gone, this one was here.

My mother carried the food to the table. "The bread's a day old, I'm afraid. And I meant to make a pie."

My grandmother looked over the platter of chicken, the bowl of potatoes, another of green beans. "It's a good plenty."

After we had taken our places at the table, there was that pause about who would say grace. My grandfather nodded to my father. "It's your house, Dan."

We bowed our heads for the blessing. It was the same one I had heard my grandfather say, but this time I understood the words.

"Our heavenly Father, thank you for this food. Bless it to the nourishment of our bodies. May the work of our hands be ever favorable in Thy sight, and we do give you the praise. Amen."

~ ~ ~

By the time I got to my grandfather's place the next morning, the lumber was laid out along the new foundation, and men were busy measuring and sawing. I noticed then something I had not noticed before: my grandmother's marigolds still bloomed at the far edge of her garden and her apples were turning red in the orchard. I thought of that picture of our bungalow being built. Maybe by apple cider time there could be another picture of my grandfather, father, and Uncle Stu—and Frankie too—atop a new house, nailing and hammering timbers and trusses together.

PUBLICATION NOTE

At the time of this writing, we are nearing the end of 2020 and my 90-year-old mother has been moved to a health care facility in Ames, Iowa, within Northcrest's larger retirement community where she has lived happily and independently for decades. This is during the second wave of the Covid-19 pandemic, and because retirement communities have suffered extensively from the disease, we're not allowed to visit her more than once a week for fifteen minutes at a time, masked and outdoors in 20-degree weather, which for my diminutive mother is more bother than not. When I call her on the phone or attempt a video chat, she is more talkative than she has ever been, though at times troubled and in pain. After a recent bout of chemo therapy, she is in remission, but the medication caused memory loss, and she has fallen three times. She now suffers a compression fracture in her back and a broken wrist, and she has no idea how these things happened. Her nurses report that she is "noncompliant," stubbornly insisting on doing things for herself, and because my family tends to crack jokes during stressful spells, we speak with pride about our tiny, noncompliant mother. Well under five-feet tall and weighing a little over 100 pounds, she subsists on vanilla ice cream and bad television. She is too tired to read. In her current situation, she wonders aloud what is real and what is not, musing that she has become the protagonist of her own story, though she is unsure what that story is.

Milk Without Honey is a novel, but one that follows the current trend in autobiographical fiction, though the first drafts of this book predate the growing popularity of that genre by decades. There are many differences between the novel and the historical record, but one of the biggest is that my grandmother left her husband to launch those boarding houses not with four children but with five. I've always marveled at how gutsy such a decision was for a woman of her time, but according to my mother, my grandmother regretted it, referring to the move to Centerville as "the worst mistake I ever made." I can't help but think it's more complicated than that. What if she had been able to make a go of it? If the country hadn't been mired in economic collapse, might she have had better luck? And if she did still return to her husband, what if she'd been able to do so under her own terms?

My grandparents remained married—fairly happily I believe—until my grandfather died in 1972, a few months before I was born. Though I never knew him, I learned he was a great storyteller, easy in his manner, kind, and musically gifted. In another era, he too might have had different options. I knew my grandmother as a shy, quiet woman who played the piano, could craft anything she set her mind to, stuffed me with her homemade brownies as well as a delectably simple "potato mash," and derided my beloved *Wizard of Oz* because "it wasn't real." To my delight, she often giggled like a young girl as I babbled to her stories about my life. One bedroom of her house was taken up entirely by dozens of antique dolls, and I often snuck upstairs to scare myself silly with a glimpse of their cracked, glassy-eyed faces staring back. Late in her life, her children were forced to move her from this house where she had lived for decades because it had become too dangerous for her to stay there alone. Her new apartment was closer to friends and medical help, but she was miserable. I remember that apartment as an impossible maze of handmade rag rugs and half a dozen enormous reclining chairs. My grandmother died soon after at the age of ninety-two. Knowing how often she was forced to move in her early married life and how desperately she tried to make a home, it's no wonder she stubbornly held onto that house and all the furniture she could. Moving again must have broken her heart.

Sometimes now when my mother reads the medical reports about her condition, she tells me she imagines she is reading these reports about her own mother. A nurse at her retirement community recently offered this advice: "At this stage you and your mother might have to make a terrible choice: Either she lives in a place where she is unsafe and happy, or unhappy and safe."

My mother began to write after the death of my father in 1987. She joined writing groups near Fountain Hills, Arizona, where she wintered in her widowhood, as well as in Ames, performing her work in front of audiences, trying out new ideas, new forms of expression. She returned often to the Green Lake Writers Conference, the Iowa

Summer Writing Festival, and the Desert Nights Rising Stars Writers Conference, among others. Her writing community quickly became a lifeline for her, as my own has become for me.

My mother has always championed my work. She sent countless postcards and phoned family members and friends to attend my readings and buy my books. Every now and then in an unfamiliar city, a woman might appear at one of my bookstore events who seems to know me. She explains that my mother sent her. My mother has many such friends. When my first book received an embarrassing review in the New York Times, my mother attempted to placate me by saying: "Well no one reads the New York Times anyway."

When my mother's cancer returned, I promised to edit her book. And as her health grew worse, I suggested we publish it. I should have done this work years earlier, but daughters are often selfish and consider themselves busy. And I hadn't quite realized how much the manuscript had progressed since I last saw it. Reading the novel now, I am struck by the power of her voice, the deceptive simplicity of her details, the beauty of her observations, her pitch-perfect treatment of drama and humor, her ear for dialog, and her sense of pacing. This, I realized, is not just a book I should publish to please my mother. It's a book that deserves to be published on its own merits. For years, my mother tried to shop around for agents, editors—any help she could get. But a Midwestern writer without connections, a female writer in the later years of her life, has a hard time attracting much attention. One wonders how many other great books are lost due to the same.

My goal: For my mother to hold this book and read the words of those who have taken pleasure in it. My hope: for the book to find more readers, reminding them of a not so distant or strange way of life.

Thank you to the friends and writers who have read this book and offered their words of praise. Thanks to the tireless Northcrest staff for their excellent care of our mother. And thank you to my family, especially my brother David Hoover and sister Lisa Carstens, who have worked so hard to help our mother transition between living situations and doctors' appointments. I've gotten the easy part, the more gratifying part, the part that returns our mother to her girlhood.

Thanks most of all to our mother for living this story and writing it so impeccably, with so much authenticity. Though knowing our mother, I can't imagine her doing otherwise.

—With love, Michelle Hoover

ABOUT THE AUTHOR

Lorene Hoover is a fiction writer, essayist, playwright, and poet. Her work has appeared in *THEMA Literary Journal*, *Rosebud Journal*, *The Christian Science Monitor*, *The Des Moines Register*, and in the anthology *Grandparents Cry Twice: Help for Bereaved Grandparents*, among other publications. She grew up near Centerville, Iowa, and currently lives in Ames and winters in Fountain Hills, Arizona. She enjoys book groups, leisurely walks, ice cream, a working television, a good view out her window, and music.

Milk Without Honey is her first novel.

For more information, contact her daughter Michelle Hoover through her website: www.michelle-hoover.com